HOLIDAY SPARKS

AN OPPOSITES ATTRACT HOLIDAY ROMANCE

TARYN QUINN

Holiday Sparks
© 2023 Taryn Quinn
Rainbow Rage Publishing

Cover Design by Jillian Liota, Blue Moon Creative Studio
ISBN: 978-1-940346-81-6

I miss you, Mom.
Christmas just isn't the same without you around.
You were the Christmas Elf to my Scrooge.

ONE

"I will not calm down!"

Darcy Tucker dropped her chin to her chest and grabbed the edge of the jewelry counter. The customer's voice carried across the entire front end. Hour eleven and a half of an eight-hour shift and she'd almost escaped. She scanned the register stations for Tom, her relief manager for the night, but of course he was absent.

"Sir, please lower your voice."

"I'm not keeping this defective bike." Shoulders that would do the Incredible Hulk proud flexed under his gray work shirt. Her lead cashier didn't flinch, but even Jaime Suarez's drill-sergeant-stern voice wasn't cutting it with this guy.

Not good.

Darcy straightened her spine and covered the distance to the customer service desk. "What seems to be the problem?"

Jaime stiffened, her fingers clenching at her sides. "I called for Tom—"

Darcy waved her off. "It's okay." She looked up at the bulging dark eyes of the man. At least two days' worth of stubble shadowed a pronounced jaw and his red-rimmed eyes were a little wild. "I'm Darcy Tucker, the front end manager. What's your name?"

"This-this woman, won't allow me to return this defective bike."

"We'll get to that. What's your name?"

"John Hartley." His chest heaved and his face was an alarming shade of red.

The name tugged at her memory. Repeat offender? "Okay, John. Just take a breath and calm down."

"I will not calm down!"

Darcy looked down at the girl's bike from two seasons ago with its mud-caked tires and worn seat. The chain sagged and the pedals looked as though they had met pavement more than once. "Do you have a receipt?"

"No, I don't have a receipt." He pointed over her shoulder. "But that sign says you can return anything for store credit. And you can look me up."

"Yes, that's correct," Darcy said carefully. "Within ninety days of purchase and as long as you paid with a credit card, we can find you in our system."

"Well, I don't have a credit card. I paid cash." His voice rose.

"Unfortunately, sir, that bike is from at least last year." She remembered because she put the display together for the sports section herself.

"Are you calling me a liar?"

The muscles in her back tightened as if they were resistance bands. "Of course not. But without a receipt and because of the current state of the merchandise, I'll have to defer to Jaime's decision not to refund you the money or give store credit. I'm very sorry, sir."

"You are calling me a liar!" Spittle flew from his mouth.

Darcy ignored the droplet that hit her cheek. She met his gaze. Even when she wanted to flinch and hand back the money, she didn't falter. That was exactly how irate customers worked. A little intimidation and most people would fold and give the refund. "What's wrong with the bike, sir? Maybe I can get the information to contact the manufacturer. It could be under warranty." The warranty was so far beyond gone. But if a white lie stopped the man from going apoplectic, just light her pants on fire.

"I don't want no damn warranty. I want my money! The gears keep slipping and my daughter broke her collarbone! I'll sue!"

Well, crap. She bit back a sigh. He was just a worried dad, but she still couldn't take the bike back. Answering to Miriam Blackstone when she went through returns and exchanges was scarier than Hulk Smash here.

"I'm very sorry your daughter was hurt, John. I know a really wonderful bike shop that could help—"

He braced both palms on the counter and leaned in. "Fuck you and fuck your repair shop."

All sympathy died an instant and ashy death. "Sir, please don't make me call security."

"Blackstone's Department Store is a fucking shithole. I'll never set foot in here again." He steered the bike away from the counter. But instead of going out the front door, he crouched over the bike and rolled it into the huge Christmas tree that stood in front of the window with all of his two-hundred-plus pounds of force behind it.

The pop of shattered ornaments crashing to the floor to the tune of *Rockin' Around the Christmas Tree* made for a macabre symphony. A loud crack and fizzle ended in a jarring silence. Every single Christmas light on the tree shorted out.

Fury and exhaustion froze Darcy tight. She looked to the man but he was already out the front door.

"Oh my God, Darcy. I'm so sorry. I tried to get him to stay calm, but—"

"It's okay, Jaime. Just call the police."

She looked up at the camera they had trained on the customer service desk. Lord knew whether it actually got a good likeness of the man. He'd been towering over them the entire time. Not a great angle. Hockey sticks, she couldn't even remember his name.

The heavy clomping of feet from all corners of the store drove one last blast of strength into her. She stalked out onto the floor. Her feet throbbed in time with the pulsing twitch in her eye. The Christmas display was toast. And there was no way she was leaving until that was cleaned up. *Son of a bottle top.*

"Miss Tucker, are you okay?"

She smiled gently at her security guard. His paper-soft fingertips lightly gripped her arm, drawing her away from the glass. He was eighty if he was a day. His uniform was still starchy and one of the red ornaments shone in his shined shoes. "I'm okay, Theo."

"Ms. Tucker, what is going on here?"

Miriam's voice was clear, cool and sharp as the jagged shards of the gold glass ball beside her boot. Darcy sighed. She definitely hated Christmas.

Hated it.

"I'll handle it, Ms. Blackstone."

Jaime came running around the counter. "No, I'll take care of it."

"No," Miriam said so softly that Darcy's internal radar went into the red zone. "Darcy is the covering manager tonight."

Jaime's chin lifted. "Actually, Tom is. Darcy was supposed to be off almost three hours ago."

"I don't care." Miriam glanced at the door. A patrol car with its twirling lights came to a stop in front of the store. "I'll go deal with this." She turned to Darcy. "You'll need to explain to me and the police just what happened."

Jaime stepped forward. "I was—"

Darcy clamped a hand on her forearm. "I'll be right behind you, Ms. Blackstone."

Miriam pivoted on her spiked heel and headed to the door.

"Darcy, let me take care of this. You have to be here at five thirty in the morning."

"It's okay. They'll need statements from both of us." She hurried to the desk and snapped out a garbage bag. "You start cleaning and I'll come back and help."

At least she could take some joy out of throwing away some of the garish ornaments.

———

With another two and a half hours under her belt, it was well past dusk by the time Darcy made the turn onto her street. The figure eight of the cul-de-sacs and their tidy townhouses and duplexes instantly relaxed her. She'd saved for over eight years to afford her house. She'd purchased one of the duplexes to help offset costs with a tenant. There wasn't one thing she had a problem with—

Her jaw turned to stone and she was pretty sure one more molar grind tonight would break it into dust.

Lights.

Everywhere.

Her house was a freaking carnival. Icicle-style in holiday white dripped in perfect lines from the gutter that ran the length of her roof. Behind the icicles were fat retro bulbs with their unmistakable LED glow. Every tree and bush, even her planting box, was strung with white lights. Santa and his sleigh had taken over her tenant's side of the lawn, and animatronic reindeer pranced in more of the viciously happy white freaking lights.

Her heart raged.

No.

No.

No.

This was her safe haven.

There was no Christmas at her house.

Suddenly the lights started blinking and *Rudolph the Red-Nosed Reindeer* piped out of her house. *Her* house.

She slammed her car door and stared.

"Oh, isn't it amazing?" Her neighbor Carly ran across the grass. "I've been watching for your car."

Too stunned to answer, Darcy watched her house pulse and flash.

"He's been working on it all day."

"What?" She tore her eyes from the house and squinted down at Carly. She was cute and soft, her blonde hair up in a high ponytail that was only one clue to her cheerleader past. "Who?"

"Ben, of course." Carly's sunny smile gleamed in the blinding lights. "I almost never see him outside in the daytime, so I had to go and see what was going on. He got me into the spirit so much I started my cookies early."

"It's not even Thanksgiving," Darcy said woodenly.

"It's this Thursday, silly."

"Don't remind me." Thanksgiving wasn't a holiday for her. It was the precursor to madness. It used to be the start of the Christmas season. Now the day after Halloween had that place of honor. She'd been listening to Christmas music for a solid month.

She was going to commit murder. With a pen if she had to.

"I was surprised to see him working so hard on the display. You never decorate." Carly patted her arm. "The Association is going to flip out. They wanted us all to do lights this year. How can we compete with this?"

"I have no idea," Darcy said. How the freaking heck would Fifth Avenue in New York City compete?

"And I had no idea your neighbor was so handy and clever. He's so sweet."

Darcy frowned. "Are you sure you're talking about Ben?"

Carly jammed her hands into her hoodie pockets. "He was outside all day doing this. The neighborhood kids even helped. He's a regular Pied Piper."

Anger welled up again. She'd loved her tenant for one reason and one reason only. He was quiet and they never saw each other. She knew his name because her rent check was, without fail, in her mailbox on the first of every month.

They rarely spoke beyond polite hellos. He was usually leaving for work as she was coming home.

And he'd ruined her house.

"Mo-o-om!"

Carly sighed. "It's bath time. Anyway. I just wanted to say wow!" She leaned in and gave her a hug. Darcy patted her back awkwardly. *Crapballs.* "Great job! The Association is going to love you this year. We're so glad you decided to join in for Christmas." A child's bellow came across the yard again. "I gotta go before Kaden drowns Abby."

Numb, Darcy watched her house. The song changed to *We Wish You a Merry Christmas* and the lights went haywire.

And then she lost it.

"Four, five, si—" Ben paused as the Christmas song fizzled out. "Shit." He pushed up the last two reps then dumped his weight bar back onto the rack and rolled off his bench. He thought he'd worked all the kinks out of the program.

He hurried down the steps and came to an abrupt halt. The lights on the porch were out. "Dammit." He swung open the door and frowned. His landlady's spectacular ass lined up perfectly with his face. Stunned for a moment, he simply stared before asking, "What are you doing?"

Their doors were side by side in the setup of the duplex. She had a pair of pliers in her hand and each of the clear clips he'd painstakingly tacked around the arched window were sprinkled across their shared deck. "I'm taking," she grunted, "down these lights."

The glow from the lights on the bushes highlighted the khaki material that hugged her ass a little too perfectly. He frowned and returned his focus to the window above. "Why?"

"Because," she snarled and pulled, "I," another clip fell and the string of lights sagged against her shoulder, "hate Christmas."

"How can you hate Christmas?" Even his cranky old Grandpa Radley loved Christmas. "Hey, stop."

"This is my house. And I will not have *We Wish You a Merry Christmas* blaring from some ridiculous speaker as lights sparkle and flash and cause seizures!"

He reached up and took the pliers from her, stuffing down a laugh. "Honestly, stop."

She looked down at him, her eyes definitely set on death ray instead of stun.

He cleared his throat. Nope, laughing would not be smart. "You're the one tearing up the siding. I tacked them in so that there wouldn't be any structural damage."

"Fine. Then take them down yourself."

"How about I just take them down on your side of the house?"

"No, take them all down. This is my house and this is my rule."

His eyebrows shot up. The librarian tone zinged him in places it shouldn't. "That wasn't in the lease agreement," he said amiably. The little pulse in the side of her neck was fluttering and her eyes were just a little too bright. She stood a few inches taller than him thanks to the stepladder. And he was pretty sure she was a minute away from a true meltdown.

"No structural changes to the house covers that, Mr. Hartley."

"Well, Miss Tucker, I hardly think a few Christmas lights could be considered structural changes."

"Oh no? There's a freaking," she widened her arms, gasping for breath, "sleigh in the yard with all—and I do mean all—the reindeer. Oh, and my house looks like a demonic jukebox!"

He wasn't sure why her rant made him want to grin like an idiot, but it did. "I like Christmas. The kids get a kick out of it and it's... well, it's cheery."

She turned on the stepladder and the whole thing tipped. Ben grabbed the first thing he could—a handful of curvy hip. She slapped her hand onto the siding for balance and stared down at him with disdain.

He cleared his throat and stepped back. Laughing would only tick her off more. The little voice in the back of his head wanted to keep going and see if she'd pull a Linda Blair. This was probably more words than they'd shared since she'd showed him the house over the summer.

He crossed his arms, digging his fingers into his quickly cooling muscles. It was a warm night for November, but not exactly muscle-shirt weather. "Look, it's getting dark. I'll take them down first thing in the morning, how's that?"

A little muscle twitched in her cheek. He could tell that she wanted to argue with him, but she finally nodded and stepped down. "Tomorrow," her chin tipped up, "please."

Now this was the Darcy he was used to. The polite, almost icy woman he bumped into at the mailbox. She was usually rolling up the driveway as he was heading to his shop. Perversely, he liked the one that had flipped out a moment ago.

"Sorry you don't like the decorations." She almost met him eye to eye even off the ladder. It was odd for him to be around a woman nearly as tall as he was. The porch light illuminated her just enough to see her gaze drop to his arm. His voice gentled. "I'm even sorrier that you hate Christmas."

"I didn't know I had to make myself clear on the subject." Her gaze tripped to the tattoos that sleeved his right arm. The sweat had faded in the coolness of the night but his muscles were still tight from his workout. "You don't seem the caroling, Christmas-is-my-secret-hobby type."

He swiped his hand down his biceps and tightened it under her obvious perusal. He was proud of his ink. He turned until the evergreen in the middle of the flames of the dragon was in her line of sight. It wrapped most of his upper arm. Most people only saw the dragon. They didn't notice that in the midst of the fire, a Christmas tree glowed bright with lights and a blue flame star at the top.

With all the crap he'd seen on this earth, one thing remained. He loved the hope of Christmas. It wasn't the religion part for him, just the hope of it. Wars had yielded one night of peace, people smiled at strangers and children reminded everyone what it was like to have a bit of simple pleasure.

"And who would be the Christmas type?"

"Carly."

He laughed. "Carly is definitely a Christmas mom, but kids have that effect whether you're the type or not."

"Christmas is ill-mannered people, impatient lines and the screams of overtired children that have been dragged to eight stores in three hours." Darcy Tucker's eyes were pinched and her mouth was now a grim line.

He swiped his thumb down the tree in his tattoo. "Christmas is alive and well no matter how awful things get." Her dark-green eyes softened and she opened her mouth to say something but he lifted his hand. As she said, it was her place. "I'll have them down tomorrow. Do you mind if I enjoy them tonight?"

She nodded slowly. "One night."

"Sorry to inconvenience you."

She snapped her stepladder shut, averting her eyes. "Thank you," she said softly and slipped inside.

Ben collected the clips off the deck and stuffed them into his pocket. It had been an unusually bitter month on the all-around. His niece was wrapped up tight with a shoulder harness thanks to a bad fall from her bike. So instead of the art lessons he usually used to keep her occupied, she was moping around his shop, Luna Hart. With any luck she'd get the sling off before Christmas.

His brother was working extra hours to pay for her medical bills, which made Brittany even more bratty. And he'd just dented his savings to buy updated equipment for the shop, so he couldn't help.

Putting up a bit of Christmas cheer had calmed him. Now he'd have to bring the lights over to the shop instead. It didn't exactly suit the tattoo parlor, but Cesar would have to deal with it.

And maybe he could finally get Brittany to smile. She liked to order him around, and getting her involved in the decorating would distract her.

He gathered the white lights that sagged from the awning and took them down because now they just looked stupid. He worked quickly. Thanks to his height and Darcy Tucker's rampage there were only a few left. He wasn't sure why she'd taken them down on his side first. He shook his head. Now the house looked as though it was winking. He made a mental note to add that into his programming ideas.

It was too bad Darcy Tucker was so unhappy about Christmas.

She sure was pretty under the twinkle lights.

TWO

Darcy watched the flicker and flash from her bed. Icicle lights divided the large picture window overlooking the cul-de-sac, ruining her favorite view. Gingerbread-perfect houses and well-tended lawns lined up perfectly. Her neighborhood was crisp and clean, so unlike the places she'd grown up in. Her mother had done the best she could, but each apartment had been worse than the last.

She'd worked hard for this view. To be able to afford her own house and her own lawn, her own space that wouldn't be taken away.

She wouldn't feel bad about Ben Hartley and his Christmas lights, darnit.

Even if they did make beautiful swirling patterns on her creamy duvet. Ben's lights were a pristine white, not the ugly neon cast of her childhood.

She rolled over and closed her eyes against the lights and the memories. She needed to sleep.

When she woke to her bleating alarm it was still dark. She groaned and drew her blankets over her head. Back-to-back twelve-hour shifts were taking their toll. In the warm cocoon of blankets, her eyelids grew heavy. Before she let herself fall back to sleep, she flipped her covers back.

The room was dark save for the cool blue numbers on her alarm. Ben must have put the lights on a timer, or shut them off well after she'd drifted off. Her toes hit the cool floor, dragging her the rest of the way into consciousness. She stumbled down the stairs for coffee and a bagel.

It was too early to focus on her to-do list. Instead she opened her laptop. A notice from her mother's Facebook account made her smile. She spent a few minutes clicking through pictures she'd posted from her latest cruise. Her mother had finally found love last year and Jerry Fontana spoiled her rotten. It was about time her mother had someone to show her that life didn't have to be all about work.

She clicked open the adjoining message and could hear her mother's voice in her head as she read about the ports and all the people they'd met. Her smile faded as she skimmed the last few lines. They were going on a couple's cruise for Christmas. They knew how busy she'd be for the holiday rush.

Her bagel suddenly tasted like cardboard.

It was fine. She'd be working the entire time anyway.

It would save her the rush after Christmas Eve closing. She never got out of there on time. And because she didn't have a spouse and children she was always drafted to work that night.

It was better this way.

Darcy closed the lid on her laptop and glanced at the clock. She was behind schedule. Routine and a lifetime of early mornings kicked in. She was ready and in her car twenty minutes later. Just as she was about to back out of the drive, she looked up. The simple Japanese Maple she'd planted when she'd moved in was the only thing still lit. The delicate branches were strung with tiny white lights, creating a soft glow. The simple loveliness reminded her of a night light for the neighborhood. In all honesty her house didn't look so bad. And if she left a few of the lights up she wouldn't have to listen to Carly and the Homeowners' Association for the entire season.

Practical.

"Shitake mushrooms." She dug out a block of sticky notes from the bottom of her bag, scribbled a note and hopped out of her car. Ben had obviously spent a lot of time on the display and it was stupid to make him take it all down. She tiptoed up the steps to her tenant's side of the porch and stuck the note to his inside door. Before she could change her mind, she rushed down the steps and to her car.

The drive to work was uneventful. Everything besides retail was uneventful at a little after five in the morning. She parked her car at the edge of the parking lot and bundled herself against the wicked wind that had picked up overnight. Today definitely felt like a November day in Massachusetts.

Blackstone's Department Store was a few miles outside North Easton. A lot of people who worked in Boston lived here. They still did a steady business thanks to the ease of shopping. The T was great for quick trips into the city, but when people had a haul of Christmas shopping to do it was much easier to do it in the suburban outskirts.

She jammed her hands into her pockets. She'd lost her gloves— again. Blackstone's was an anchor store to a massive strip of shopping centers. The parking lot was large and without cars to break the wind, her cheeks and neck were frozen halfway across the blacktop.

She waved to her fellow department manager Kelly Brennan, who held the door open for her.

"Hiya, babe. Cold enough out here for you?" Kelly's bright-blue eyes danced above the fat knit scarf that covered half her face.

"Five a.m. is inhuman in the winter. I went to bed it was dark, and it's still dark," Darcy muttered.

"Just think, we might get to see an hour of daylight after shift today. Miracle!"

"After the day I had yesterday, I doubt it."

Kelly winced. "I heard about the tree and that customer."

Surprised, Darcy adjusted the strap of her purse. "How'd you hear?"

"Text from Jaime. She felt so bad, Darc. If that stupid Tom had come up like he was supposed to then he would have had to deal with it."

"Yeah, well, if Tom had to deal with it then there might have been punches thrown. That man was no joke yesterday." She rubbed her hands together. "I felt really bad for him. His daughter fell off her bike, so he was truly just upset about that."

"Yeah, but what did he actually think would happen when he brought it in?"

Darcy sighed. "I don't think he was thinking."

"Obviously."

"Between the cops and the tree it was bedlam." Darcy shook her head as they hustled down the hallway at the rear entrance of Blackstone's. "The lights pulled free and fritzed out, singeing a few of the branches." For a split second she'd wished the tree had gone up in flames.

No, not really. Okay, maybe a little, but then again dealing with a fire would have been a lot worse.

"I can't believe he took out the tree. I always miss the good stuff."

Darcy laughed. "I just wish it hadn't been when Black Widow was on," she said under her breath.

"Oh man. Jaime didn't tell me she was on last night."

"Yep. It wasn't pretty. I didn't get out of here until nearly seven last night. Then I go home and find my house lit up like Christmas on an acid trip."

Kelly laughed. "You are terrible. I don't know anyone that hates Christmas more than you do."

"Yeah well, unfortunately I lost my cool with my tenant last night and now he knows. In detail."

Kelly bumped the employee break room door open with her butt. "You didn't."

"Oh, I did. You should have seen his face." She looked down at her bag, fussing with the zipper. She felt bad about laying into him. He'd been shocked and possibly a little amused that she hated

Christmas. People who weren't in retail just didn't understand how bad it could be.

"I don't think I've met your tenant."

Darcy sighed. "He was perfect. He pays his rent on time and I never hear a peep out of him. Well, until the holiday music came blaring out of some speaker he had set up under the porch. Kel, you should have heard the songs. It was awful."

Kelly snickered. "I can only imagine."

"I think I would have handled it better if I just hadn't had to deal with the Black—" She stopped as Kelly's blue eyes widened. "The Blackstone's store catastrophe," she said quickly.

"I'm still not happy with the tree, Ms. Tucker. I'd like you to concentrate on that with Mr. Anderson this morning. The store must look perfect. My parents are coming in tomorrow and the decorators aren't available to come back and redo the tree before Friday."

Darcy hung her head. More tree crap, and with her favorite manager. Perfect. "Absolutely. I'll take care of it."

"I want it to be classic and fun. Santa will be coming in for the children all weekend."

"On Black Friday weekend? Are you insane?" *Shut up, Darc.* But that was the worst weekend even to contemplate doing something like that. People would be tripping over themselves for the sales, not bringing their children in for Christmas pictures.

"The directive came from my father, Ms. Tucker. I want this store perfect." Miriam left the room, her stilettos clicking over the sandstone tiles.

"Are you crazy?" Kelly tugged her into a chair. "I can't believe you said that."

"I can't believe they're doing this for Thanksgiving weekend. Are they out of their minds? It's going to be chaos in here." Darcy gathered her hair away from her face with the hair tie she always had on her wrist. Putting her hair up before six a.m.? It was not going to be a good day.

"I know," Kelly sighed.

"Deep breath," she muttered and stood. "And now I'm off to deal with Grabby Gary."

Kelly dragged her in for a hug and patted her back. "Stab him with your box cutter."

"Don't tempt me," she said with a laugh. She swiped her badge to log in for the day and hit the floor. Darcy was responsible for the front end and the jewelry department officially, but at Blackstone's titles meant less than their words. She'd worked every department in the twelve years that she'd been with store. And gearing up for Black Friday meant all hands on deck. The only good thing was that it would go by quickly.

She waved to the cleaning crew who were buffing the floors as she headed for the front end. The store didn't officially open until eight and there was plenty to do before then. She opened the cash box door with her badge. A brunette of indeterminate age sat at the long metal desk, candy-apple-red kitten glasses balanced on the tip of her nose. A half-dozen cash drawers were stacked and ready for the cashiers. "Morning, Mo."

"Hiya, sweet cheeks. How goes it?" Her fingers never paused over the calculator keys and the rubber tipped thumb on her other hand flipped through receipts.

"Another day of eternal bliss."

Mo snapped her gum with a grin. "I don't think your definition of bliss and mine are the same. Mine? Daniel Craig kidnapping me for a secret assignment."

Darcy shook her head. "Your bliss definitely wins."

She took her mini-tablet from the slot and signed it out, then looked over the schedule loaded. One thing she did like about working for the Blackstones was the toys. Miriam had upgraded them from walkie-talkies to a network of handheld computers. She smiled at Mo on her way out the door.

"Remember, Daniel Craig doesn't have security clearance for back here."

"Spoilsport."

Darcy laughed and tapped through the various screens, noting that there were no callouts so far, but the day was still young. Her feet knew the store by heart, so she continued to look through the day's schedule while she walked.

"There's my gorgeous Darcy. How you doin', kid?"

Darcy's easy smile tightened. "Morning, Gary." Shock and dread roiled in her stomach, her smile long gone. "What did you do with all the decorations I had on the tree?" She'd worked for an hour to get them back on.

"Miriam took them down before I got in. She said it looks too much like a Hallmark card. Which, if you ask me, is the point of a department store tree, but what do I know?"

"I couldn't agree more." And that was a first.

He moved closer, his arm brushing hers. Hugo Boss cologne assaulted her nostrils and made her eyes burn. Did he bathe in it?

"She wants us to put these up instead." He toed an open case of lights. "I don't understand them myself, but what do I know, you know?"

Obviously not much—you know? She took a step to the side and away from his aura of cologne. "These?" She flipped the top box and groaned. A listing of typical songs made her want to weep. She unearthed the end of the string and plugged them in.

Instead of the real songs, a horrible electronic facsimile of *Come, All Ye Faithful* filled the air. It sounded like a sample from a Casio piano that her mother had given her one Christmas. She'd lose her mind if she had to listen to that for the next month.

Gary leaned into her. "See, they play tunes. Pretty cool."

Darcy leaned away and set the lights down. She ignored the hovering Gary and looked up at the fifteen-foot spruce that they'd had delivered the week before. It still had a root ball that would be planted along the side of the store in the spring. Very green and very PR of her boss. The heavy ceramic pot was hidden by a huge red skirt with a fluffy white cuff.

It was lovely. Truly. And as much as she hated Christmas, she didn't want those tacky lights ruining her store.

All she could think of was her neighbor and his ingenious, if annoying, display. Now that would make a statement. She looked at her watch, then at the tree again. "I'll be right back." She headed to the back of the store where Miriam's office was and knocked.

"Come!"

She squelched the need to roll her eyes. Imperial decree, how comforting. "Ms. Blackstone, I was wondering if I could talk to you for a moment?"

Miriam looked at the slim gold watch on her wrist. "I have a few minutes."

"I was thinking about the tree. The lights you chose aren't exactly Blackstone material, if you ask me."

Her eyebrows rose as she sat back and steepled her fingers. "Oh, really?"

With an inward wince, Darcy kept going. "No, I think that once you saw them on the tree and heard the unfortunate songs, you'd feel the same. I was wondering if I could check in with a...friend of mine. He might be able to help us out." Now that she was actually in Miriam's office Darcy wasn't sure it was a good idea, but she forged ahead. It was too late to back down now. "He's done a neighborhood display that's quite impressive."

Miriam tapped her lips with her scarlet-tipped nail. "How impressive?"

"My homeowners' association is fairly taken with him and he loves Christmas." Darcy's voice strengthened. Surely she'd be able to get Ben Hartley to help her. If she begged. And allowed him to keep his display up on her house—if a little more...tempered. She tucked a strand that had escaped her ponytail around her ear. "Since we have an abundance of managers on right now I could go back to my house and be back within forty minutes." She'd probably wake him up. "At most an hour."

Miriam nodded. "You were here late last night, I think that would be fine. I appreciate all you did to salvage the tree. What is this person's name?"

"Ben Hartley."

Miriam slid her tablet in front of her and typed quickly. "Make sure all the receipts go to Maureen in the cashier's box. Normally I'd make sure to hold you to a budget, but this has to be handled as expediently as possible. Within reason, Ms. Tucker. I trust you."

It took all the power she had in her to not to let her mouth drop open. Did the Black Widow just tell her that she'd done a good job? "I appreciate that."

"Well, don't just stand there."

Ahh, there she was. Darcy resisted the impulse to snap a salute and turned on her heel. She checked her watch. It was barely seven thirty. She was tempting fate with this scheme, but there was no way she'd be able to pull off a Blackstone-worthy display on her own. Maybe she could take half the rent off as a Christmas present. Her bank account could handle a one-month hit.

She sent a quick message to Gary's unit to leave the display alone and to cover for her per the boss's decree. She lengthened her stride and gathered her things, stashing her tablet in her locker before signing out. Now she just had to figure out a way to convince Ben Hartley to be her Christmas savior.

THREE

Ben pulled the pillow over his head, trying desperately to ignore the incessant buzz of his alarm. He flung his hand out but it wasn't his alarm. He squinted at the clock. "That better be 7:50 p.m.," he muttered.

The shrill ring of his doorbell finally scraped at his consciousness. "Fucking fuck." Whoever was leaning on it as though it was their job was going to pay. He'd been up sketching until after three. And it was his goddamn day off. He fumbled out of bed and nearly walked down the stairs before he remembered that he slept in the raw.

That was one way to get rid of whoever was at the door.

He tugged on a pair of workout shorts and a shirt before shuffling down the stairs. When the blasted bell went off again he growled his way to the door and swung it open. "What the hell do you— Oh, for God's sake, I promised I'd take down the lights today, not at eight in the fucking morning."

His landlord winced and twisted her fingers together. "Actually," she pointed to the note on the door, "I left that this morning before I left for work. And now I have an even bigger problem."

A jaw-popping yawn was his first answer. "Look, Miss Tucker—"

"Darcy."

"Darcy." He decided he liked the way it felt on his tongue. And that was dangerous. He should have stayed in goddamn bed. His landlady's teeth chattered as she held the collar of her coat up under her chin. Sunny yellow hair whipped around her face. In the searing light of day, her pretty eyes were even more captivating. And that little tidbit was a sure sign that he needed coffee. Now. "Do you want to come in?"

She was going to saw her damn bottom lip off before she answered, so he reached out and took her arm, dragging her inside. "It's freezing."

"Didn't you get the email that it's winter?"

Ben looked down at himself and then back at her. "I was sleeping. You're lucky I have this on."

Those evergreen eyes widened and a bit of his grumpiness slipped away. Maybe she wanted a better look at him. "I know, and I hate to bother you, truly. Truly," she repeated. "I know we kind of got off on the wrong foot yesterday."

He crossed his arms over his chest. "Actually, I think your foot might still be in my ass from yesterday."

Darcy brought her cupped hands up to her lips and blew into them. "Can we sit for a minute?" She looked around his living room. "I mean if that's okay."

"It's your house," he said, stepping down into the living room. Three large boxes of decorations were clustered around the fireplace. "You made that clear yesterday."

She hunched up her shoulders. "I had a really awful day yesterday, and it's no excuse, but I came home to find that Christmas threw up on my house." She sighed and sank into his couch. "It wasn't my finest hour."

He sat across from her. Luckily he'd actually picked up the house yesterday. Christmas decorating always equaled a major overhaul inside and out. "No, but I should have mentioned it to you, I suppose."

It was her house, as she'd explained. But he did use LED lights to keep down the cost. Anything he did wouldn't have increased her electricity bill more than a few pennies.

She slid off her coat. A lightweight gray sweater hugged her shoulders and scooped low on her neck to emphasize her collar bone and elegant neck. *Not the right time to notice all of your favorite spots on a woman, Hartley.* Especially this woman.

Darcy pushed up her sleeves and leaned forward. "Speaking of those decorations."

He sighed, leaning back and lacing his fingers over his belly. "I told you I'd take them down."

"No, actually. I'd left you the note to leave most of them up. Maybe tone them down to a more traditional look, but keep most of them."

He sat up. "Why the change?"

"Once I'd calmed down I thought about how much work you'd done and how much Carly loved your decorations. She's the head of the beautification program for Oakwood Gardens."

She was too much. She didn't care about the work he'd done. "So now you're in with the bigwigs and all is fine?"

"Not the bigwigs, just the Association. They're always on me to decorate with the rest of the neighborhood. You saved me the trouble."

"Glad I can be of service."

She blinked. "I didn't mean it that way." Darcy rubbed her forehead. "Look, you're brilliant."

Ben laughed. He didn't need his rather lovely landlady to stroke his ego. "It's okay, I get it. Since you hate Christmas, it's a tough sell."

"Hating Christmas is a major understatement, but it's for a good reason."

Ben quirked his brow. "There's no good reason to hate Christmas."

"I work retail—at a department store."

Ben leaned forward, resting his elbows on his knees. "Okay, you might have a reason to dislike it, but hate it? C'mon. With all those happy kids and the—"

"The miserable mothers with children they've dragged to every store since they opened? Or would I love the kids that that are let loose in the store like it's their own personal playground? Or better yet, that parents think the toy department is a daycare and can just let the kids play there unsupervised while they shop?"

"Okay," he held up his hand, "I get it." He had a feeling there was still more to it.

"And that brings me back to why I'm here. A holiday hiccup that is making my boss twitchy has landed in my lap and I'm wondering if you could help me."

"Oh yeah, the deal is sweet as hell from where I'm standing, darlin'. You deign to let me keep up my ornaments and now you want a favor?"

Darcy's chin dropped to her chest. A hank of lemon-blonde hair fell out of her messy twist. Texture was his downfall and between the fluffy soft sweater and her finger-grip-worthy hair, he should jam his hands under his thighs before he did something stupid.

She made a huffing sigh sound. "I'm not doing this right."

Ben stood up. The urge to brush her hair back and tell her everything was going to be all right made him itchy. "What's the problem?" He hated to see anyone miserable. That was all. But then again, she hated Christmas. And that just wasn't natural.

She peered up at him through heavy bangs. "I need your talents at the store. Can you do what you did to the front of my house on a fifteen-foot spruce?"

He rubbed at his biceps. "Wait, did I just hear you right? You want me to come to your store and—"

"Make Christmas explode all over my front end. Money isn't an object." Her words came out in a rush.

Ben grinned. The absolute misery on her face was epic. "And I get full creative control?"

She nibbled at her lip again and Ben wanted to brush his thumb over the full, raspberry-colored flesh. And that wasn't going to happen. She'd probably bite his finger off.

Darcy lifted her chin. "Within reason."

He had a feeling within reason meant micromanaging him into a safe little display like every other store. "Sorry, darlin'. I'm not interested."

She stood quickly. "Okay, wait. You can have as much creative control as I can get out of my boss. How's that?"

He drummed his fingers on his arm. Her eyes drifted to his chest, then his arm and back up to his face. He tucked his hands under his arms. And again, her eyes strayed to his sleeve of ink. Maybe the good little girl next door liked tattoos. "I only have today."

"That's perfect, because I need it done today."

Maybe it was her earnest eyes that were just a little wild, or maybe it was the fact that she'd swallowed her pride to come and ask him to help her, or maybe he was just insane. He heard himself say, "All right. Turn your pretty butt around and go back to work. I have to go shopping."

Her mouth hung open. "Pretty butt?"

"Well, it is. I got an eyeful when you were tearing apart my work."

"I—" She cut herself off with a shake of her head. Dammit, she was cute when she was all flustered. "All right. It's Blackstone's Department Store."

He whistled. Blackstone's was old family money. "Really? And you want me to decorate it?"

"I need Christmas perfection and that seems to be you."

He laughed. "Now it suits you that I'm a Christmas freak?"

"Yes."

"Just like that?"

"Look, Ben...can I call you Ben?"

"I think you should at this point."

"This very unruly and very miserable customer tore through the store with his daughter's bike and took out half the front of the store's decorations. Desperate doesn't cover it."

Ben's breath stalled in his chest. That was coincidence. "Daughter's bike?"

She tucked her hands into her sleeves. "Yes. He lost it. I just can't get over how upset he was."

"And you didn't call the cops?"

"We did, but we don't have a good image of him on our video surveillance. And in the commotion, I didn't get a license or ID."

Ben rubbed his biceps again. Christ. It couldn't be. "Okay, darlin'. Why don't you go back to the store. I need to get some supplies and my computer."

"Why?" She shook her head. "And stop calling me darlin'."

He smirked at her. It kept slipping off his tongue. "Now that I know it bugs you, I definitely won't."

Her eyes flattened and her nostrils flared.

He smiled wider. "You're kinda gorgeous when you're mad."

She made a disgusted snort and turned. "If I wasn't in such a bind I'd—"

"You'd what?"

She picked up her coat and stuffed her arms into the holes before he could think about holding the jacket for her. "I'd have the lights off the front of the house so freaking fast."

"Temper, temper, Miss Tucker."

"I hate Christmas!" She stalked to the door and jerked it open.

"Hey, wait."

She swung around, a lock of hair falling into her face before she blew it away. He grinned at her and plucked a scarf off his coat rack. "It's freezing out there." He wound the simple navy fleece around her neck.

Her eyes widened before she muttered a thank you as she stomped down the stairs. He watched her go. Superior ass didn't even cover it.

Ben swiped his hand over his jaw. He was well past scruffy and headed for beard. The tattoos and the rough face probably wouldn't go over well. He climbed the stairs two at a time and started planning as he quickly shaved and showered. He scrubbed a towel over his hair and body, swiping it over the fogged up mirror. His hair was too shaggy. It was all right when he was beardy, but now he looked like a boy band reject.

"Stupid baby face," he muttered, splashing aftershave on with a hiss. With a grunt, he slapped the towel over the bar and went into his bedroom to pick over his clothes. After five minutes of staring, he grabbed his usual jeans. He was not dressing up for this woman or her store. For fuck's sake, it was bad enough that he'd shaved.

He dragged a long-sleeved thermal down from his armoire, then tucked it back in. No way was he covering up his tats too. It was going to be hot as hell in the store. He pulled on a black t-shirt and snaked his skull belt through his loops. He wasn't changing for any damn woman, let alone one that worked for corporate America.

He gathered the soundboard he'd soldered together. He'd been working on an in-house treatment like his outside setup. It was modified to play a softer version of the songs, and could be synchronized with other lights in the house. From the banisters to the mantel to the tree, it could all be set up to play songs in a series or as few as one an hour. Perfecting the kit had taken years.

He was going to give it a test drive in his house, but the department store would be a better plan. With a little ingenuity he could show it off and maybe sell a few kits by next year. He stacked his soldering tools into his soft-sided duffel and tucked in the board and his laptop. On the way, he stopped at a home store and bought bulk lights. Unsure whether she needed more than that, he tossed a few animatronic deer in the basket along with beach ball-sized ornaments.

If there was one thing Ben knew, it was color. He'd gone to school for graphics but had fallen in love with the tattoo gun halfway through his sophomore year. He'd altered his degree to hone his talents in illustration and color theory. And decorating an arm was no different than decorating a tree. It was all about the right colors. He grabbed balls in varying tones of gold and red. The purples and blues were too close to the shade of a spruce's green needles. The warm colors would make for a better pop.

A few more oversized ornaments and he moved on to the fat retro lights. He liked the blend of new and old. The red and gold would make for a great traditional palette that would work well for a department store.

A few hundred dollars in the hole and he was back in his truck. Blackstone's was close to the big box stores on the strip. He pulled in and parked around the back of the store. A beefy guy hopped off a forklift and tipped his sweaty ball cap back. "Can I help ya?"

"I'm looking for Darcy Tucker."

He looked from Ben to the truck and back. "For?"

"Christmas display."

"Oh yeah. She mentioned to be on the lookout for you. Need help with the supplies?"

"If you have a pallet jack and a big bin I should be able to back up the truck and we can do it in one go."

The guy looked as if he could bench-press him with a truck to spare, but when he grinned, his face transformed and he looked like a happy puppy. "Can do. I'm Petey."

"I'm Ben."

"Pleased to meet ya." Petey scratched his head and replaced his hat. "You're going to save Darcy's bacon. Our boss is on a rampage for the store to be showroom-ready for the holiday weekend. Even has a Santa coming in to appease the kids as the parents shop."

Ben loved Christmas but there was no way he was coming out after Thanksgiving in the mess of retail hell. He did most of his shopping online.

"Well, let's see if we can get the store in fighting shape. I'll pull around the truck."

Ben backed in and the two of them unloaded his supplies in a few minutes. Petey jacked up the bin and pulled the crate in for him. "Miss Blackstone will freak if I let you do it. Store policy and all."

"Ah." Ben nodded agreeably and followed the burly man. He chattered on aimlessly and Ben listened with half an ear. He was already plotting the store makeover. And adding to his shopping list.

The department store wasn't exactly on his top ten places to shop so he was unfamiliar with just how large it was. The Christmas tree dominated the front. Even without all the garlands and lights she was magnificent. Full and a deep green. Very much like Darcy's eyes.

He frowned.

Not why he was here. He had a job to do, and he needed to keep his eye on the prize. Perfecting the display would go a long way in helping out his financial situation. The lights had started out as a bit of fun, but if he could get that moving maybe he'd actually be able to build his house fund again. He didn't regret going into business with his best friend Cesar, but he hadn't been prepared for just how much of a financial drain it could be. Especially when his partner preferred partying to worrying about overhead.

He came around the bend and the entirety of the registers and shoppers came into view. It was still early in the day but there were a few people shopping already. He spotted Darcy speaking to a coworker. The minute she realized he was there her entire body language changed. She actually stood taller, if that was possible. It was a novelty to have a woman be nearly the same height as him.

Made for a few interesting ideas.

No.

No ideas.

As she walked toward him, he decided a few ideas weren't necessarily a bad thing. Her legs were distracting as hell. She had a loose-limbed grace that he rarely saw outside the models that frequented his shop. But without the arrogance.

And the pull he felt was annoying. She ate up the length of store between them. Slim navy pants made her legs look even longer. There wasn't an ounce of gawkiness to Darcy Tucker. In fact, she had more curves than he'd originally thought. She hid under shapeless clothes most of the time.

"Thanks so much for coming, Mr. Hartley."

"Considering you've seen me before my toothbrush, I think Ben will do."

Her friend joined them and her eyebrows rose at his last statement. The silent conversation that ensued between Darcy and her coworker was fascinating. He had a feeling Darcy was going to have some explaining to do. And he decided he liked that she blushed and wouldn't look him in the eye.

The little dark-haired woman peered up at him. "So, Gigantor. Are you going to fix our store?"

Ben smiled wide and held out his hand. "I'm sure going to try. You are..."

She blinked and shook his hand. Her dark eyes took in his tats. People couldn't help but look. The bright red, green and blue ink was meant to attract attention. Cesar was a genius with ink and used him as a test subject to try out the brighter and deeper inks that were coming out. "Jaime."

"Pleasure." He clapped his hands together and both women pried their eyes away from his ink sleeve. "Now, where's all my power? I've got work to do."

Darcy kicked into action. Those long legs headed to the bare tree. "I see you have some materials already."

He followed her over to the tree. Keeping his eyes at the back of her head was far more difficult than it should have been. "Yeah, just some foundational things. I'm going to need more. So what exactly can I get my hands on?"

Son of a bitch, he needed to stop thinking about his hands and this woman.

Intent on her body language, his chest tightened. Darcy linked her fingers together, her knuckles going white before her grip loosened. She tapped one thumbnail against the other. His girl was nervous.

"Right. Well, I—" she turned to him, "I just have to say one thing first. I really don't know how I'm going to thank you, Ben. I can finesse a schedule tighter than a marine sergeant, but you ask me to do this and... Well, I'm just lost."

Surprised that she'd own up to not being able to do something, he jammed his hands into his pockets. He didn't want her thanks. The minute she mentioned the broken bike and ragey behavior, he'd had a really bad feeling. Blackstone's was right around the corner from the shop his brother worked at. And just how many little girls had a bike injury out there right now? There had to be a few. It was a common thing for kids—he was just being paranoid.

His niece Brittany was the only thing that his brother John cared about. Add in his already dodgy behavior and it wouldn't surprise him to find out his brother had done something stupid.

Now Ben just had to figure out a way to make sure John didn't get into any more trouble.

He punched up the wattage of his smile, pleased to see a return bend to her distracting mouth. A little too pleased. She had a mouth made for a long, hot kissing session followed by a bottle of wine and a whole lot of sweaty foreplay. And damn if he didn't like foreplay.

Foreplay and Darcy Tucker was not a good idea. He had to remember that.

"I'll just put you down in the 'you owe me one' column and collect later." Fucking hell. He was not going to collect later.

She tucked her hands into her sleeves. There sure must be something interesting about her shoes, because she kept staring at them. "Sounds good to me."

He laughed. "That was a joke."

"No, I pay what I owe. And this is business."

"It's a favor for a friend."

She finally met his gaze. "We're not friends."

That only made him smile wider. "We could be if you did more than grunt at me on your way into your side of the house."

Her eyebrows rose. "You're no better."

"We're both to blame."

She took a deep breath. He watched her consciously relax her shoulders and draw in two breaths. "I will be deeply in your debt if you pull this off."

"Darlin', there's no if. This will be awesome."

The corner of her mouth twitched. "Confident."

"This is my element."

"I seem to remember."

He couldn't stop grinning at her. "Let's see if I can outdo our house."

Her pupils dilated and her gaze dropped to his mouth. "My house."

She certainly wouldn't let him forget. "Your house," he said with a shrug.

She took a step back. "I'll leave you to it."

Before she could disappear, he touched her arm. The softness of her sweater lured him closer. "What am I allowed to play with?"

She licked her lips. "Sorry?"

He quirked a brow. "What areas do you want me to work on besides the tree?"

"Right." She cleared her throat and looked around. The front end was neat and tidy but as sterile as a doctor's office. "The surrounding platform. The chair that will have Santa on it. And the checkout stations. Just make sure that the cashiers can move around easily and that customers won't trip."

"I'll concentrate on the tree area and do the register stations after hours. What time do you close?"

"Oh." She looked more than uncomfortable. He was going to impress the hell out of her and he couldn't wait. "Nine."

"Okay, I'll work on the big stuff. I'll need to go out for more supplies. Do you want me to bring you back lunch?"

"I—" She looked so surprised at such a simple kindness. There was no way a beautiful woman like her wouldn't be used to male attention. It just couldn't be possible.

"I have to get something for myself anyway," he said, trying to alleviate whatever it was that wouldn't let her ask for help. Knocking on his door must have really burned her ass.

"You don't need to trouble yourself."

"We'll need to talk over the plan sometime. Might as well eat while we're doing it." Christ, what was it about her that made him want to push for more? *Not good, Hartley. Not good at all.*

"I brought my lunch."

He shrugged. "Suit yourself."

She unearthed a small electronic tablet from a holster at her hip and hugged it to her chest. "If you need anything just flag me down. I'll be running around most of the day."

He nodded and moved to the bin. Petey had brought him up a ladder and a shaggy-haired man hovered along the sidelines. He was average in every way except the way he watched Darcy. That, Ben didn't like.

At all.

FOUR

Darcy left Ben to work, but throughout the morning she kept finding excuses to go back and check on him. She found herself smiling when she caught him with ropes of lights around his neck and shoulders. His black t-shirt was faded to charcoal and didn't quite stay down around his hips. Not when he kept reaching up to tuck lights in whatever strategic way he seemed to have devised.

A heavy black belt gripped his hips and somehow seemed to accentuate how tight he was. Everywhere. Smooth skin peeked above the belt. Even the little flashes of flesh were muscled. And a tiny corner of a tattoo peeked along his side.

It made her want to push up the shirt and see what it was. It looked like words. Just what sort of words would Ben Hartley have tattooed to his flesh forever? A woman's name? A line of poetry? A sarcastic saying that fit his lightning-quick wit?

And he was tireless. He was up and down the ladder, painstakingly wrapping branches in some pattern only he seemed to know. Petey, their receiving manager, kept coming out to see the progress.

Ben seemed so at ease with everyone. He had Petey cracking

jokes, Jaime bringing him bottles of water hourly, and every cashier that could get away from their register volunteering to help him.

Was he giving off some sort of special pheromone?

That had to be why she was just as pulled to him.

She forced herself to look back down at her schedule. The midshift was coming in. She had breaks to cover and Jaime needed to take her lunch. And she had to sit down with Ben and talk about the design.

"Where did you find him again, Ms. Tucker?"

Darcy looked up from her tablet at Miriam's voice. The woman was a cat. "He's my tenant."

"I thought you lived in the suburbs?"

Darcy clicked off her screen and snapped it at her hip. "I do. I own a duplex."

Miriam looked over at the tree, then back at her. Her lips were pinched and her ice-blue eyes were even cooler than usual. "How long did you say he'll be here?"

"Is there a problem?" Darcy didn't like her tone.

"He's blocking the front end with all his...paraphernalia."

Judicious as always, that was Miriam. Darcy bit back a sigh. "Actually he's going to be here through the day and will be doing the big changes during the overnight."

"He's staying in the store all night?"

"He's doing us a favor, Ms. Blackstone. I'm making myself available for whatever he needs. He's only charging us for materials. Not his time or his expertise."

Miriam's shoulders went back and her spine stiffened. Even more than usual, and that was a miracle of anatomy. "I understand that, but he's..."

Darcy tipped her head to the side. "He's..." She wanted her to say it. All her life she'd had to deal with people like Miriam Blackstone. She'd had to fight for every promotion in this store because she'd come from nothing. Just because Ben had tattoos all down his arm and looked a little dangerous didn't mean he wasn't trustworthy.

For goodness' sake, the man was the poster child for Christmas and easy smiles.

"I don't know him," Miriam finished. "You'll be here with him all night and you'll be responsible for anything that happens. I want this store perfect for tomorrow when my parents arrive."

"Oh, it will be."

"See that it is, and I'll make sure my parents know you were the lead on the project."

Darcy's skin tingled and all the hairs on her arms stood up. No matter how much she hated Christmas, this was a perfect opportunity to show she could be assistant manager. Christmas was a marketing tool. Nothing more.

"You won't be disappointed."

"Since you'll be here late, I'll have Mr. Anderson take your morning shift. I want you here when my parents arrive at one o'clock."

"Understood."

"And, Ms. Tucker. I can't stress how perfect this needs to be."

Darcy nodded. She'd been looking for a way to prove herself and this was it. She hurried over to Ben, who'd shrugged on his jacket. On her way by she motioned to her watch and made the get out of here sign to Jaime. Her lead cashier waved her off and went back to the register. The woman was worse than she was about taking breaks. But Jaime was hourly and breaks were mandatory. Darcy was salaried.

Salaried in retail was tantamount to slave labor. She stopped beside the ladder. Ben stood above her and from this angle she could see more of the tattoo, but still not enough to read it. She seriously had to stop looking at him as if he were one of her dark-chocolate caramel swirl ice-cream bars. It was getting ridiculous.

"Ben?"

"Yeah?"

"You have your jacket on and you're back on the ladder."

He looked down, the corner of his lip tipped up in amusement.

"You're observant, Darcy. Did I ever tell you that?" He buried his arm into the limbs of the tree until his face disappeared into the foliage.

What the heck was he doing? Looking to take a sap sample? She rolled her eyes. "Aren't you going out for supplies?"

"Yes ma'am. I just need to figure out how much more I need. This spruce is a big mother." He climbed down quickly. The squeak of protest from the ancient ladder made her nervous. There wasn't an ounce of fat on the man, but he was...well, strapping was a good word. Dense muscles flexed and flowed under his skin. His jeans hugged massive thighs.

Don't think about his thighs.

"You've got lights wrapped around every branch. Is it going to be too much?"

"No, I need to manipulate each branch for the music."

"How?"

He stepped down to the floor. He was so close she could feel the warmth of his skin and the tantalizing scent of pine and leather swirled around her. "Do you really want to know how I use channels and create the sectors that the music will be manipulated through?"

Wow. Vastly underestimating her neighbor's prowess with electronics was going to get her into trouble. Bad boy look and brains to spare? Nope, not at all good for her peace of mind. "Engineering degree?"

"Nope, my degree is on the streets, darlin'. I learned everything I know from friends and acquaintances, with a side of trial and error."

Her belly twisted. She knew all about on-the-job training instead of college, but for this kind of thing? She wasn't sure it was a good idea. "This is going to work, right?"

He tapped the tip of her nose. "I'm going to blow you away."

She folded her arms. "You're a cocky one."

"Nah. Just aim to impress the pretty girl."

She could feel the heat of her cheeks. Damn fair skin. "I need Mr. and Mrs. Blackstone impressed, not me."

"Yeah, but you're the one I want to impress." He clicked his boot heels together and gave her a snappy salute. "I'll be back and you are going to sit down with me for at least twenty minutes and eat."

"I'll try."

He cuffed her wrist with his forefinger and thumb. "It's going to be a long night, Darcy. You'll need your strength."

Gosh, she hoped he couldn't feel her pulse hammering away as though it were a rabbit on meth. One touch and she was a frazzled mess. And he was right. She needed her strength to get through the night. And dinner. "Is that offer still open?"

His lids lowered. The hooded look made her think of anything but the possible sandwich he was bringing back. "Which offer is that?"

"Food, Ben."

The smile was slow and anything but innocent. "Of course."

The entire night with him? She was so freaking screwed.

Oh yeah.

Screwed.

"I'm getting a sub from Lou's. Want a hot or cold one?"

The Lean Cuisine she had stashed in the freezer for emergencies paled in comparison. "Meatball," she said before she could stop herself. She should have asked for a salad or anything else but a sauce, meat and cheese explosion of garlic.

Her mouth watered at the thought. She rarely allowed herself to have takeout. It was just too expensive and she was saving to build a deck off the back of her house. She patted her pockets.

"I got it."

"The least I can do is buy lunch."

He nudged past her, giving her ponytail a yank. "I got it. If I can get you to sit with me for twenty minutes and talk it will be well worth it."

"This isn't a date."

He threw a grin over his shoulder. "Oh darlin', you'd know it if we were dating. You'd be smiling a helluva lot more." He disappeared beyond the jewelry counter.

Her nails dug into her palms before she realized it.

"He's right." She turned to find Jaime beside her. "I bet you'd be smiling like that damn fish Dory that my daughter can't stop watching."

"Oh sure, that's attractive. Dory's the vapid, forgetful one, right? I think not. Besides, he's too cocky. What the heck would I do with a guy like that?"

Jaime's eyebrow rose. "If I have to explain it to you, then it's been way too long."

Darcy jammed her fisted hands under her arms. "He's my tenant."

"He's smokin' hot."

"Looks aren't everything, Jaime."

"When he looks like that and is giving off signals that every tower in the next five towns can read? Yeah, that's when you pounce. Like now. Or better, when the store's closed and you're alone."

"There are cameras!"

"Not everywhere and you know where the blind spots are."

"Jaime."

"What? You think the bedding department hasn't been violated six ways to Sunday? Please."

"And that would be six of the many reasons why I wouldn't do that." Darcy shuddered. Working in a department store was never boring, that was for sure. How many times had she run people out of the dressing rooms? It might have been hot in the movies to make out in the little confined spaces but the reality of it? Ugh. Not so much.

Jaime lowered her voice. "You need someone to put you up against the wall and give you a good orgasm."

Her eyes widened as she looked around. "You did not just say that."

"I did. Look, my Michael may not look like the god of Christmas trees and ornaments but he knows how to make me scream. And you are overdue. Why don't you just see what happens? If it doesn't amount to anything, who cares?"

"I have to live next to him."

"I know for a fact that you can pretend to like just about anyone, Darcy. You haven't killed Gary yet."

She tipped her head back. It wasn't a good idea. At all. She tugged the sleeves of her sweater down, hiding her hands. "How about you go on break?"

Jaime sighed. "You can avoid it all you want, babes. But you know you're interested. I've watched you watching him all day."

"Nosy much?"

"Looking out for my girl," Jaime corrected. "Have some fun. All you do is work and go home. What's wrong with having a little fun with Christmas boy?"

"Because he's Christmas boy. He loves it. I can't stand it. I'll strangle him with a string of lights when he tries to convince me to decorate at my house."

Jaime laughed. "So you're thinking about him in your house, huh?"

"Oh, shut up."

Ben loaded the last of his purchases into the back of his truck. If he did this for real he'd have to look into buying in bulk. He'd made a pit stop at the computer store for another board. He'd modified one to run the lights at the house, but needed a bigger circuit board to control all the different strings of lights he'd needed to use at the store. The tree was fucking huge. And he'd need to play around with the program to make it work.

He'd made sure that each layer of lights on the tree was even so he could make a few different patterns. And because he was a glutton for punishment, he'd tagged a song out of his personal playlist. A non-holiday tune to make Darcy smile.

Masochist was the word of the day.

Christ, he went out of his way to get her to smile. How fucked was he? She was his landlord, for God's sake. Hadn't he learned anything with Jess? He'd done the roommates deal to save money and they'd broken every rule about being friends. Hell, they'd christened every room a dozen times. They couldn't get enough of each other at first.

At first.

Then came reality. Living with a woman was hard. The compromises to live with a friend were hard enough. He'd had roommates for most of his life, but living with a woman and becoming intimate was completely different. Bad habits came out, shitty days couldn't be ignored, and if he wanted to just work on sketches and be in his own space, he was the bad guy.

No.

This so wasn't a good idea.

He slammed the tailgate.

Okay, so they technically lived separately. If he wanted time alone, he had a whole wall between them.

And that was idiocy talking.

A wall didn't mean anything when two people were dating.

No woman he'd ever been with had known the meaning of personal space. And he couldn't bear to disappoint someone he was involved with. Because he was an idiot. He was overthinking everything.

It was a sandwich. And it was an evening. Even if everything about her made him want to pull her in and see how she fit. That was hormones talking.

After Jess he'd needed a break from the opposite sex. Then it just got easier to stay in his routine. Workouts, messing with the Christmas lights, the shop. Everything but going out with his friends.

He pulled into Lou's small parking lot. The cars were stacked fifteen deep in a lot that was barely big enough for six. The shouts from inside and the hot punch of garlic on the air made his mouth water. Lou's was a dive to beat all dives. And the strip of shops it was in was moving into the high end of trinkets, wine and boutiques. All except Lou.

Deli paper lined the walls with buckets of crayons nailed beneath. Red booths that had been there since the opening when he was a kid were jammed against every available wall and the deli counter was chin-high. Specials were taped up along the front breadboard and torn down daily. The signs were made by Lou's kids, and now grandkids.

"Hey, kid," Lou yelled when he spotted him.

"What are you doing slinging hoagies, old man? Where's Dom?"

"My useless excuse for a son is hurling up his toes."

Ben winced. "You poison him?"

"Hey! There's nothing but excellence under my roof, kid."

Ben laughed. A Red Sox cap sat backwards on Lou's bald head and his sauce-splattered t-shirt hung off his shoulders as though they were a hanger. Lou was all bones and angles, but behind the counter he was magic and fluid grace. He had bread sliced open, yeasty sourdough warring with the garlic as two guys Ben didn't know scrambled to keep up with the owner.

"Can I get a meatball grinder and a Philly steak to go?"

Lou made quick work of the food and wrapped the sandwiches in foil then deli paper. "I haven't seen you in a few weeks."

"Work's been kicking my ass."

"Inking up all those hot girls." Lou waggled his bushy eyebrows. "They like those little designs above their butts. Nice."

Ben grinned. Tramp stamps, as they were lovingly referred to, never quite fell out of favor. The curve of a woman's spine and the hollow at the sweet spot of her back was a damn sexy place to accentuate. And it wasn't a hardship for him to do. But women forgot how sensitive it was to use the needle around bone. Fleshier girls didn't mind, but the rail-thin ones—well, more than one had walked away with a smaller design than intended.

"The only downside of my job is the pain."

"True that." Lou lifted his sleeve to show off a skeleton in a Red Sox uniform clutching the World Series trophy. "This hurt like a bitch."

Ben took the food. "Because you're goddamn skin and bones. You should come in and let me retouch that."

"What and jinx my team?"

Ben rolled his eyes. "I've got the lucky touch, didn't you get the email?"

"I'm too busy feeding you vultures. Next!"

Ben texted Cesar and with no emergencies on the horizon, he maneuvered his way out of the clusterfuck that was Lou's and back to Darcy. No—back to the store. Back to the job at hand. The job just happened to have a lovely side benefit, that was all. He tucked their food into his messenger bag with a fistful of napkins from his console.

After a quick unloading with Petey, he braved the store. He slung the bag over his head and behind him as he stacked the materials next to the base of the tree. He had a good eight hours of work ahead of him and that was if everything went smoothly.

He scanned the room and found her. Her hair tumbled around her shoulders as she pushed it back with a harried look. She was bent over her little tablet, flicking through screens as Jaime ticked off something on her clipboard.

Looked like trouble to him.

He dumped the last case of lights and walked over to the customer service desk. It was quiet at the store. A little after two in the afternoon, it was a wasteland compared to what it had been right before lunch.

"No, he's over hours."

"What about Henry?"

"He's not really ready for being on his own, is he?"

"I trained him," Jaime said, "and I can watch for any issues."

"Okay, call him in. He's eager and wants hours."

Jaime scribbled something.

"Hey, ladies."

Jaime smiled. "Hey, Gigantor." She sniffed. "That's not cologne, doll. What do you have?"

Darcy leaned forward and took a long sniff. "Better than cologne." She looked up, her eyes widening. Her cheeks flushed and the freckles he hadn't noticed before flared. She cleared her throat and drew back. "You brought me food." She moaned. "I can't get away."

His chest tightened at the soft sound. Is that what she'd sound like under— No. He was here to work, not think about Darcy and the sounds she made when she relaxed. Hell, would she relax even during sex? She was always so wound up.

"Yes, you can." Jaime pushed her portable tablet away from Darcy. "It's as close to calm as we're going to get."

"But we've got three callouts."

"And we're dead. Go, before we're not. Gary is on the floor so if something comes up I'll call him."

"He's useless up front."

"Yeah well, as long as we don't have another customer like bike guy, then I don't need him."

Ben's fingers stiffened on his strap. Petey had shown him pictures from the day before. He still wasn't positive it was his brother, but damn, it had been a mess. "C'mon, Darcy. We need to go over what's happening the rest of the day anyway. Can't let me go unsupervised, can you?"

Darcy sighed. "No, I suppose I can't."

Man alive, this woman didn't know the meaning of the word teasing. He pulled his bag over his head. "I've got a meatball grinder. Darcy, eat me," he said in a faux Muppet voice as he wagged the flap.

She huffed out a laugh. "All right." She slid her tablet into her hip holster. "Call me if you need anything, Jaime."

"Go." When Darcy hesitated, Jaime shooed her. "Go and leave me be. I'll call Henry."

"I'm going."

Darcy rounded the counter and snatched the bag out of his hand. "I could eat the bag I'm so hungry."

"Lunch room?"

She nodded to the back. "Near receiving. We have a little employee room."

He followed her and again she outstrided him. He picked up his pace and caught up to her. "Racing?"

She slowed down. "Sorry. I should probably get one of those fitness watches. I have to walk a dozen miles in here a day."

"Who needs the gym?"

She smiled. "The day I get a desk job is the day my butt goes to the gym."

"Do you want to do something different?"

"No. I've been here since I was seventeen. I love it." She tapped a code on the door. "Most of the time." She backed into the door, swinging it open for him.

"What about you? I mean I know where you work, but do you love it?"

"I own my own place and don't answer to anyone. Works for me."

"Doesn't surprise me."

Two round tables and an old picnic table filled the room. A pair of vending machines and an ancient fridge lined the back wall. She set his bag down and went to a small locker tucked behind the door. "Soda?"

"Yeah, diet whatever." She pulled out money, crossed to the machines and set two bottles of Diet Coke on the scarred table. "What doesn't surprise you?"

"You don't seem like you're a rules kinda guy." She hooked her leg through the bench-style seat of the picnic table.

He unloaded their food. "I tried the employee thing. I even apprenticed for five years at a studio, but Chuck wasn't interested in doing anything but the tats in the books." He peeled back the paper and, finding sauce, slid it her way. "None of his own art. I was getting more clientele than him by the end." He shrugged. "It was easier to leave than ruin a friendship."

She unrolled her grinder carefully, her eyes closing as the scents of garlic and sweet marinara sauce floated up between them. "Jealousy has a nasty side effect."

He grunted. Both for her visceral reaction to the food and his past. A reputation was all an artist had in the tattoo business. He did the trade shows, even inked a few celebrities when he'd lived in Boston. But he liked having his own place. Close enough to go into the city for conferences but far away enough that he could take it easy and hone his craft. He'd built up a good name, but his space was small. Just him and Cesar.

She tore off a quarter of the sandwich and lifted it to her mouth just as a chime came from her hip. "Dammit." She put it down, licking the tips of her fingers. "Just five minutes, that's all I ask."

"You're allowed a break, Darcy."

"Yeah, tell that to Gary."

"I will."

She looked up, her deep green eyes wide with surprise. She glanced back down at her tablet and tapped something before tucking it back into the bag at her side.

"Staying?"

"He can handle it. We have things to discuss."

He tried to hide his smile.

"No smirking. I did it for work."

"Of course."

She took a big bite and muffled what sounded like an ode to Lou before swallowing. "So, tell me what's going on for the rest of the day. Miriam's bugging me hourly for an update."

"I got what I needed from a few stores. Once I'm done with the gear and program the lights, we'll be in business."

She pulled a little notebook out of her pocket, this time with a pen. "How do the music and the lights work?"

"I can program the lights with most songs. It works with the beats. I hardwire it into the music that plays on the overhead and tell it only to recognize certain songs."

"Really?" She picked at a meatball and wrapped it in a string of cheese before popping it in her mouth.

He grinned, rubbing at the corner of his mouth that mirrored where extra sauce settled on her.

She blushed and picked up a wad of napkins.

Too bad.

He would have liked to brush it away for her.

More dangerous ground.

Her little tether to the store chimed four more times during their meal. Each time, the idiot Gary couldn't make a decision without her. If Ben wasn't mistaken, Gary was checking up on her. On the last ring she finally stood up. "Evidently a half hour is too much to ask for."

He tucked the remnants of his sandwich into the wrappers and collected hers. "Go ahead. I'll be fine."

"Are you sure?"

"The world is obviously going to fall apart without you."

She sighed. "I do actually have two days off. Most of the time."

"Tell me you don't come in on your days off."

"Sometimes it can't be helped."

"Delegating is an art form. They need to learn about it."

"Yeah well, until that magical day happens I'm the It girl. Especially with Black Friday coming so fast."

"I'll make sure the store is ready for that crazy holiday. I promise."

She stopped beside him and leaned down, brushing a kiss along his cheek. "You don't even know what a lifesaver you are."

He turned his cheek until their mouths lined up. She sucked in a breath, her eyes such a deep green it didn't seem natural. Everything inside him said take. The soft sweater that hugged her, the pale hair that kept sliding from its bindings, her lower lip that she couldn't stop licking—all those textures lured. Add in the ocean-fresh scent of her and he couldn't resist. He leaned in but she drew back, tucked her hands into her sleeves and hurried to the door. "I'll just let Miriam know the plan."

Damn. He lifted a foot out, straddling the bench seat. Was she running because she wasn't interested? Or because she was just as attracted as he was? "I'll see you later."

"Right. Um, right. I'll find you later."

Then she was gone.

And he had work to do—a lot of it.

FIVE

DARCY RUBBED THE HEELS OF HER PALMS TOGETHER FOR THE eighth time. Her palms were so itchy she was pretty sure she was going to go insane. Okay, so what if it was only when she had to come up to the front end of the store? It didn't mean anything.

She passed the tree stand. Ben wasn't there. Her heart rate stuttered into an easy rhythm with a side of disappointment. Ri-freaking-diculous. She needed to calm down and stop thinking about him. It was her imagination that he was going to kiss her in the break room. Garlic breath, exhaustion and this sudden surge of attraction were making her crazy.

That's all there was to it.

Period.

"Hey, Darcy."

She stopped. Now she was hearing things.

"Down here. I'm hiding from Tiffany."

She wished she could hide from that particular cashier herself. She crouched down and saw Ben sitting cross-legged against the wall in the shadows of the tree. There was a small storage cubby hole there. He had a string of lights set on the half wall so he could see what he was doing. "What are you doing back there?"

"I told you. Hiding." He lifted a small tool that looked like a pen. "And soldering." He waved her in. "She'll see you and then she'll know my spot."

She laughed. Ridiculous was the word of the day. She dropped to one knee. There was no way she was crawling under the tree in her wool pants.

That half grin tipped up his mouth. "I won't bite. C'mon."

"I have work."

"No, you're off shift. You're mine."

She swallowed. "Wh-what?" The way he'd said *mine*. Not right in any way.

His grin spread into a smile. Just how flame red were her cheeks? "Your Miriam Blackstone came over. She told me that after three you were all mine for the day. She wants this tree beyond perfection."

Of course that's what he meant. She'd gotten the same orders, but she assumed that just meant she would be required to be in the store. Not helping him. "You don't really want my help, do you?"

He crawled forward, caught her hands and dragged her across the slick floor until their knees touched. "I really do."

She ducked her head and pushed a branch away. Dust bunnies and pine needles scattered around her. "I can't believe you just did that."

He patted the spot beside him. "The little throwback from *Valley Girl* is a little too much to take. If she asks me one more question I'm going to strangle her with the pink stripe in her hair."

Darcy giggled, stifling it as soon as she started, but it was too late.

"What? Do I speak the truth or not?"

The laugh broke free. "Yes. Gosh, yes." She leaned against the wall. It was cozy and out of the way and so much cooler. A sweater had not been the way to go today. Of course if she'd known she'd be working a twenty-four-hour shift she would have dressed differently.

PJ's perhaps?

What did it matter, she was a wreck already. She slid down the wall until her knees were higher than her eyes. "I'm just going to take a nap. Can you wake me when it's over?"

"If you sleep like that you'll be in traction. I'm good at a back massage, but not that good."

"You gotta stop saying stuff like that," she said on a groan. Then wanted to curl into a ball. Outside voice—that had definitely been her outside voice.

"Why?"

"Because." She struggled to sit up. "Because, heck. I don't know why."

"Are you seeing someone?" His gaze dropped to her mouth then lifted to her eyes. "Not into guys?"

She laughed. "I'm into guys."

"I'm too tall?"

She laughed again. He was far too charming. "That's just mean. Do you know how often I meet a guy that's taller than me?"

"Do you know how often I meet a woman I don't have to crick my neck to kiss?"

Her palms tingled again, right up to the tips of her fingers. "You want to kiss me?"

He set the board and the soldering tool aside and spun around until he was facing her. His knee pressed into her thigh as he gripped his crisscrossed ankles. "Oh yeah."

"Now?"

"Definitely now."

What if someone saw them? The tree wasn't that big, was it? "I taste like garlic," she blurted.

He leaned closer. "I love garlic."

The pads of her fingertips flattened into the cool floor. She moved in until his scent wrapped around her. Spruce from spending the day with the tree and a lingering hint of cinnamon stuck to him. They lined up like puzzle pieces, shifting and turning until they fit. His hand moved beside hers on the floor, not quite touching. His nose bumped her cheek, then nuzzled against hers lightly. Soft as cashmere, his bottom lip brushed hers. Sweet and innocent, the kiss was everything he shouldn't be.

Ben was the last man she pictured herself kissing, let alone hiding behind a tree with. But he kept the kiss light in every way. The tip of his tongue flicked along her lower lip and his other hand came up to cup her cheek.

His thumb coasted along the crest of her cheek as his fingers slid into her hair. She hitched in a shaky breath and opened for him. He sucked her tongue lightly before covering her mouth completely. All the while his fingertips slid through the strands of her hair along the side of her face and gathered them into his hand. He gently stroked her hair and continued the easy and thorough exploration of her mouth.

Too overwhelmed to do anything but go along for the ride, she curled her forefinger over his on the floor. She rose onto her knees, bumping into his long legs. He tipped his head back to keep the kiss going and she opened her eyes. She pushed away his overlong bangs, coming up for air and a moment of sanity. His long neck was corded and so intrinsically male.

Stubble dotted his neck, swirling around his Adam's apple. He swallowed hard as she dragged the pad of her thumb down the column, taking a precious breath that her lungs couldn't possibly handle. He opened his eyes a fraction. The glittering heat in his deep-brown eyes trapped the rest of her breath in her lungs. She settled her hands on his shoulders, tracing her thumb over his fluttering pulse.

Reassured that she wasn't alone, and more importantly that she wasn't doing it wrong, she lightly trailed her fingers along the solid muscles between his neck and shoulder and up. He'd obviously shaved that morning, but his stubble was already there, pricking the pads of her fingers as she traced the strong line of his jaw. She followed the indent of his chin to the shadow under his lips. The patch of hair was slightly softer there. As if he hadn't quite gotten all of it on his shave.

She touched his lower lip and he opened for her, tipping his chin down to take her fingertip between his teeth. His steady gaze was disarming. Patience was there, but it wasn't the only thing. No, there was a wealth of heat too.

For her.

She couldn't stop the curve of her own mouth. When had a man ever looked at her like that? The power of it ticked her heart rate up until her breath quickened. Wanting a taste, needing a taste of something that thrilling, she pressed her mouth to his. The tip of her tongue found his, but instead of falling into the kiss this time, she teased him.

Gaining confidence, she did the sucking this time, drawing him deeper into her mouth. Sliding against the side of his tongue, she was the explorer. Cinnamon burned her tongue the deeper she went. He'd been chewing gum recently. So ordinary, but the peppery bite kicked her into gear. She drove her fingers into his hair and sealed her mouth to his.

He slid his arm around her waist as the kiss went deeper, pulling her tighter to him. She'd never been kissed like this in her life. As if she were precious and delicious at the same time.

Her name buzzed from his throat before she felt it on her tongue. Deep and growling with an edge of something more. Something she'd never tasted. Men didn't get riled up for her. She simply didn't incite passion.

She pulled back.

But instead of letting her go, his even white teeth nipped at her chin as his fingers gripped her hair and dragged her back down. Slanting lips and clicking teeth replaced the first kiss. He pulled her into his lap until she straddled him and he cradled her against his chest.

Her palm slapped against the wall and the tree shuddered as her shoulder bumped a branch. Still he didn't stop. And she was too far gone to care where they were. The kiss went from meadow-picnic sweet to black silk sheets and sweat within moments. The puzzle pieces had snapped together, flush and perfect. And it was amazing.

His grip was almost bruising, but it only pushed her harder. Made her want more. She could feel the press of his zipper against her slacks. The bulge of a man not the least bit unfazed by her kiss. No, there was clear want as her heart slammed against her chest. Was it just hers? The tumultuous beat couldn't be just her.

The tablet at her hip beeped. She pulled back instantly.

"Don't." He sighed and tipped his head back when she unlocked it and flipped open the cover. She was officially off shift, but it was Miriam. She was coming up to check in with them.

"I'm sorry. It's Miriam."

He shimmied his hand up between them and cupped her face, pushing her back and yet holding her tighter at the same time. "Her timing blows."

"I shouldn't be making out in the corner like a teenager."

He nuzzled along her neck. "Being bad feels good though."

She closed her eyes. Gosh, did it ever. But this was her career on the line. "You make it a habit, Mr. Hartley?"

He leaned back, the cool white of the lights accentuating the shadows and angles of his face. He was incredibly good-looking. The kind of good-looking that made a woman feel as average as copy paper beside him. She tried to shimmy back a little but he held on tight. "I haven't wanted to touch a woman for a few months until just now."

She searched his eyes. The deep brown had little tiny flecks of gold in them. Almost imperceptible until she was—oh, say three inches away. "Bad breakup?"

"You could say that."

"I..." She what? She couldn't say she didn't want him to kiss her again. That was a damn lie. "I liked this."

"I think like is an understatement." He shifted under her and her eyes widened. That quirk to his mouth was back. "Sorry."

"Uh huh."

He leaned up with a laugh and nipped her bottom lip. "I really do like kissing you, Miss Tucker."

She couldn't stop the smile. "Ditto."

His fingers tightened along her hips, riding the curve of her backside. "I like it a little too much, but I'm not exactly for voyeurism."

"Too bad." Shocked that it came out of her mouth, she detangled herself. "I—"

He laughed. "Kinky manager. Oh darlin', we'll have some fun."

She stopped. "We will?"

He paused, then nodded. "I think we both could use it."

"Even if I hate Christmas?"

"I'll change your mind."

"You are one cocky man."

"Just about making you have some fun. I'm good at it."

Of that she had no doubt. "Work first."

He curled an arm around her waist, brushing his fingertips along the curve of her rib cage. "Authoritative women are hot."

She pushed him back, delight beating down the doubt. "Well, then you'll love me."

His smile slipped a bit. "Do you need to go talk to boss lady?"

"She's going to come up and check on us in a few minutes."

"Then let's get to work. I have most of the lights set up on switches. Now we just have to follow the grid I made up." He scooted back, grabbed a graph notebook and handed it to her.

She crisscrossed her legs, settling beside him again. The tree was to scale, and was damn close to a photograph representation. The man was talented. He had each bough sectioned off with a string of lights and labeled with letters. Along the side there was a paragraph of code that meant less than nothing to her. She turned the page and found scribbled notes and a rough sketch of the registers with more lights labeled. The fat retro ones were obvious and the tiny twinkle lights were so effortlessly weaved throughout she didn't even know how to react.

Through Ben's eyes, the store would be beautiful.

He was going to put her on the path of assistant manager. With Christmas.

The irony wasn't lost on her.

She turned to him. "This is amazing."

He took the notebook with a smile. "It's going to be amazing when I get it set up."

She brushed her hand over his shoulder. "Let me just brush a little of that confidence off you, Ben."

He rolled onto his knees. "You want this store to be the best. I'm the best."

"What did I say about that confidence?"

"I've been working on this for years. Now I get to implement it on a grand scale. I'm going to make this so good you'll be able to feel Christmas right into your bones. And you're going to love it."

"It's just lights." But she wasn't so certain anymore. The pure determination in his eyes was contagious. She straightened her shoulders, not willing to back down. "You're going to make my career, Ben."

A little of the cocky swagger faded as he changed course and slid out the back of the tree. "I hope I change your mind about Christmas at the same time."

She followed him. The moment was lost. Because of her. But this was about business and she had to remember that. "What do I need to do?"

"I'll head back up the ladder. Why don't you work on the bottom branches? I've got it sectioned off into four." He handed her the notebook and climbed the ladder with an armful of the retro lights.

She'd been doing grids for displays for years. This would be easy. She hoped.

She pushed back her sleeves and wished for a t-shirt like Ben. Of course the entire store was clothes. It wouldn't hurt her budget too much to buy a t-shirt. "Let me just run and get something I can move in."

Hurrying through the store to the women's department, she snagged a shirt and, on impulse, her favorite brand of jeans. She needed a new pair anyway. After checking out and a quick change she headed back to the front end. Jaime met her at the jewelry counter.

"Look at you. All sexy and sassy."

Darcy frowned. "Jeans and a t-shirt is sexy and sassy?"

"They are when you have legs like that. How is it that you have legs up to your ears anyway?"

"Don't pout, you get to be tiny and dainty. I'm the Amazon."

"Yeah, well Wonder Woman was an amazon and that worked out for her."

She pulled her ponytail over her shoulder and smoothed the pin-straight strands. "Yeah, that's me." Nine hours of work left her hair limp and lifeless. No matter what product she put in it, it still ended up lying like a limp dishrag by the end of her shift. And she still had another six to eight hours to go.

"You are, *mija*. It's going to be a long day. Are you sure you're going to be okay with him after closing. All alone?"

"Yes. I'm not worried about that."

Jaime's eyebrow lifted. "Oh?"

"He's perfectly safe."

"Safe enough for stubble burn and lips that look like they were chewed on?"

"Jaime," she said with a groan.

"What? I know the look of a woman well loved. Just be careful, love. That boy has the kind of grin that will make a woman forget how to keep her panties on."

"I thought you wanted me to live a little? Didn't you just tell me to enjoy him a few hours ago?"

"I did. I'm sort of shocked that you actually took my advice."

She was too. But nothing about the last day and a half had been normal. Ben was right, it felt good to be a little bad. When had she ever kissed a man impulsively? Heck, she usually had to go out with someone at least a few times before she even entertained the idea of a kiss, let alone crawled in a man's lap.

"I've been with men like him. Fun is what you need."

Darcy could feel her face flaming. "I'm not going to do anything stupid."

"I want you to do something stupid. Something fun and stupid with lots of orgasms," Jaime said on a whisper. "But I also know how overwhelming a sexy guy can be. My Michael got me into tons of trouble."

"Ben's..." Well, she had certainly taken a chance kissing the stuffing out of him under the tree, but that was it. She wouldn't be careless. She didn't know how to be careless. "Ben's here to do a job."

"He's going to do a job on you. Enjoy it and I want details."

Darcy sighed. "I've got to get back."

"Go."

She quickened her step, faltering when she caught sight of him on the ladder, his upper half buried in the tree. She could do this. He was just a guy. Even if he was a guy who loved Christmas.

SIX

THEY WORKED TOGETHER WELL. DARCY TOOK DIRECTION AND
had an innate ability to find the most efficient way to do things. He
could see why she'd been promoted through the ranks. By the time
the store was preparing for closing they had the tree wired up and he
had a tentative circuit to try out.

Next to her boss, Darcy seemed positively friendly and warm.
When Miriam had come out to check on them the laughing Darcy
had disappeared. Within two minutes she was back to the remote
woman he was used to. The woman he hoped to banish again before
the night was over.

The chattering Tiffany tried to stay after her shift, but the
nighttime supervisor for the cashiers put the kibosh on that.
Fortunately the girl left before he could use a string of garland to
strangle himself. He was used to dealing with people in his line of
work, but a tat took three hours to do at most. Seven hours of Tiffany
was too much for any man to take.

And the fact that Darcy took a little too much joy in the torture
left him eager to work some payback into their evening. The store
emptied out and they were more than halfway finished with the

swags of decorations for the registers before the last employee left. These would be on a separate channel to play on a loop from one register to the next as programmed songs came through the sound system.

He was anxious to try it out. Now if only Darcy didn't fill out a damn pair of jeans as if they'd been made for her he'd be further along with the register setups. She slid behind him, her chest brushing against his back as she reached for the edge of a wreath.

"Sorry, can't quite..."

He turned into her, making sure his chest slid across hers as he reached for it. He unhooked it from the plastic L-bracket. "Is this what you need?"

The soft skin of her underarm brushed against his. She was so pale, dusted with toffee-colored freckles on every inch. Every inch that he was more than willing to explore. A night of counting her freckles would be a welcome project. Instead of backing off, she moved into him, her thigh sliding between his so denim whispered against denim. He rather liked having a woman line up with him. There was something to be said for a tiny woman to make a man feel big and powerful, but this way? This woman with her surprising curves?

In dress clothes she looked tall and professional, even a little untouchable. In a pair of jeans she was miles of curves and mouthwatering temptation. He groaned as she lifted her knee and bumped his balls lightly.

"You're not playing fair." He glanced up to the black orbs in the ceiling that probably had video cameras going at timed intervals. He'd like nothing more than to boost her onto the counter and find out whether she was a pretty bra type or she had a no-nonsense kind that would hold up to a day's work.

He didn't know which one would turn him on more.

And there lay madness.

She wasn't his usual type of woman. She was softer in some ways, but still there was something about how she held herself away from people that made her even more intriguing. She was stiff and formal with her employees. She seemed to relax only around Jaime. She watched everything. He wasn't sure if she was taking it all in or cataloging it for dissection and an efficiency overhaul.

And she liked to watch him.

He'd felt her gaze on him all night.

And he'd been half hard since they'd been locked under the tree together.

She batted long, light lashes at him. "Were there rules? I wasn't aware of any."

He growled, hovering an inch from her mouth. Her makeup had faded away long ago and he found that he liked her fresh face. More freckles had bloomed along the ridge of her nose and cheeks. Hell, they were all over her. Even on her lips.

Yeah, he wanted to count them, wanted to paint her entire body with his tongue to see just which ones would line up with spots that made her sigh or moan. His buttoned-up and remote landlady was missing again. In her place was a woman he wanted to get to know in every way possible.

"Maybe there should be," she said softly. "Maybe I'm not ready for someone like you."

He searched her face. The tension that had bowed tight between them snapped like a frayed rubber band. "Someone like me?"

"I can count the number of men I've been with on one hand."

He arched a brow. "What makes you think I can't do the same thing?"

She leaned against the cubicle-like structure that walled in the registers and folded her arms. Arctic Darcy was back.

"Okay, so maybe I've had a few more relationships than that. But whatever this is, it's just us. It's different than any other thing between anyone else we've been with because it's us."

She relaxed, letting her arms drop before taking his hand. "I didn't mean to insult you. It's just... Well, it's been a while. I work a lot and I don't like to mix work with..." She trailed off. "I'm not saying any of this right." She stepped into him, again her knee nestled between his. "I like this feeling. I want more of it. Does it have to be complicated?"

He shook his head. It didn't have to be. He'd hit the mother lode with this woman. Incredibly sexy and she wanted to just see where it went. No pressure. He brushed her cheek with his, the corners of their mouths touching briefly. "Let's get this done and I'll show you just how uncomplicated and fun I can be."

She drew in a shuddering breath. "Sounds like a plan to me."

Unfortunately the close quarters made for creative ways for each of them to torture the other. And he found that he liked tacking up lights for the camera and behind the counter he found ways to brush against her, smooth his palm along her ass, tangle up their legs until she was giggling around him.

He liked her laugh.

Wanted more of it.

Wanted to taste it even more.

By the time they finished the registers he was so wound up he was ready to drag her off to a corner and kiss her until breathing was optional. They agreed to take a break since he had to test the circuits he'd created and he needed to connect the control pad to the program he wrote. She brought him back to the furniture section and he spread out on one of the coffee tables.

Hip-deep in code, he didn't realize how long she'd been gone until the quick shock of cold on his neck made him flinch. She held out a bottle of soda with a knowing grin. "How's it going, genius?"

"Almost got it."

"Good, because you've been poring over this for an hour."

"Oh shit. Really?"

She nodded and covered her mouth as a huge yawn overtook her. "Definitely. It's after midnight."

He stretched his arms out and gathered everything. "I think we're good to give it a try."

She took his mini-laptop and left him with the circuit boards. "Let's get going."

Darcy caught herself mid-yawn again. She'd worked on a few outstanding displays she never seemed to have enough time for during her regular shift but kept an eye on Ben. He was focused—frowning over his screen, pushing back his hair, jamming his pencil between his teeth. Very distracting.

He looked massive and yet somehow comfortable on the floor. With all his bulky muscles, he was oddly graceful. And more than able to sit in one spot without moving. He didn't have a fidgety nature, which was probably key since he had to hold weird positions for long blocks of time as a tattoo artist. She couldn't stop staring at his long, graceful fingers.

And that was the path to destruction.

Every time he touched her, she wanted more.

She'd never been a sexual creature before, but around him she couldn't stop thinking about just what he could do with those artist hands. And maybe he was right. Whatever she'd done and whomever she'd been with before—it wasn't Ben.

It was a heady feeling.

And downright hard to define. She was used to meeting someone, dating, waiting at least a few weeks before she thought about taking a man to bed. With Ben, all she could think about was getting him against any available flat surface. After that kiss earlier, she could only imagine what he'd do if he was focused on her with unlimited space and time.

Just her and just him.

"So tell me, Darcy. Why oh why do you hate Christmas?"

"Do we really need to go over that again?"

"Yep. Because I'm about to make you love it. And I want to know why it sucks so hard in your opinion."

"Making it beautiful won't make it less of a pain in the butt. I've never really been all that into it. My mom always worked through the holiday. And for her, Christmas was her only day off. It was hard to celebrate when she was so exhausted. So it just became another day. And then I started working retail, and that was all she wrote."

"But wouldn't it be the day to celebrate that you got to spend time with your mom?"

"She was so exhausted she usually slept most of the day."

He frowned. "You didn't leap on her bed with bouncing blonde pigtails and demand to see what Santa brought you?"

She stopped a few feet away from the front of the store. "Santa made a really small pit stop at my house, and when I figured out he didn't exist, well...I couldn't see making my mom spend unnecessarily on me."

She hadn't meant to say so much.

What was it about Ben Hartley that made her do things that were so out of character? He didn't need to know her sob story. What a way to kill the mood. He moved into her space and she froze. Now he was going to feel sorry for her. She was asking for a night alone the way she was going.

He lifted her chin with his finger. There was sadness in his deep, dark eyes but there was also a steady calmness. "I come from a single-parent home too." He kept his eyes open as he leaned in. The kiss was sweet and slow. Like their first kiss, it was spring-breeze soft. Her eyes drifted shut and she fell into his taste. He kept it light and she followed his lead. Content to drift on the gentleness in his touch, she sighed when he drew back.

"I'm going to make you love Christmas again."

She reached up to cup his face. "How about you make my store look like Christmas on crack and we'll be even."

He pressed his forehead to hers for a moment then stood back. "Okay, we've got some testing to do."

She followed him to the displays, placing his laptop on the counter at the customer service desk. Ben had taken over a corner of it to set up the wireless circuit boards. It was the largest area and he could get at it easily if anything happened through the holidays. The things he could do with Bluetooth technology were as close to amazing as she'd ever seen.

He hopped over the desk and disappeared behind the tree to plug in whatever it was that he'd created back there. He flipped the switch and the front end literally glowed. Every light was on and without the rest of the store's halogens it was even more pronounced. The tree was majestic with the classy white lights and huge, colorful ornaments he'd bought. Instead of the greens, purples and blues that had been on the first tree now it was all gold, red and orange. The only kaleidoscope of color was the trunk of the tree. He'd lined it with colored fat retro bulbs.

Their LED light was bright in a strangely flat way and served as a perfect base for the warm LED whites he'd bought. She thought it would dull the color of the tree, but it only accentuated the golds of the ornaments and made the whole room pop. If she didn't know better, she'd be expecting a warm fire to be crackling bedside the tree.

He'd used a cooler-toned white light to decorate the evergreen wreaths behind each register. Fat silver bows hung from the bottoms with holly berries instead of ornaments. It was pure class. Even without the light show, the man knew how to create an amazing space. She lifted herself onto the podium Jaime used to watch over the cashiers and direct traffic on the busy days.

Ben was behind the customer service desk at the back wall, directly across from her. He was intent on his little shells of electronics and tapping on his laptop. Suddenly an updated version of *O Holy Night* shot out of the speakers, making her heart jump. Christina Aguilera's unique voice soared.

The displays fluttered then steadied. The tree light took on a swirling pattern in time with the soft song. It was as lovely as fairy wings. Surely something so elegant couldn't be designed so easily. Just how much work had he put into this? The song drifted into a jazzy piano piece with a gospel chorus and the tree flashed and came alive.

She couldn't stop the smile.

The man was good.

In fact, it was even better than she'd hoped for.

He came around the counter and walked to her as the song changed to Elvis. He crossed the floor and held his hand out to her. She laughed and shook her head. He circled her waist and pulled her down from the podium, drawing her into an easy box step. She laughed. "Where did you learn to dance?"

"Single mom." He dragged her hands up and around his neck and laced his fingers at her back. Thigh to thigh, they swayed to Elvis' smoky voice as he sang about a blue Christmas. The lights on the tree slowly faded in brightness, went back to full light, then twirled down the length of the tree and took a slow trip around the entire display.

"Impressed doesn't cover it, Ben."

"I told you I'd make the store amazing."

"You did." She laid her head on his shoulder and let him lead her around in a soft swaying circle. The song ended, but instead of another Christmas one, a heavy rock power ballad remake made her giggle. The powerful and gritty guitars flooded the room and amazingly the lights shimmered in time to the drums. "How?"

"Any song can be programmed."

She played with the ends of his flyaway hair and rose onto her tiptoes. "George Michael is probably wincing right now."

"I like it."

Darcy laughed. "I'm never going to think of *Careless Whisper* without thinking of this."

"Good." He lowered his head and the dance of lights disappeared behind closed lids as he kissed her. This one wasn't sweet. It was as gritty as the guitars that gave new flavor to an old song. Her fingers bunched into his shirt, her nails into the hard muscles of his shoulders as she held on. They'd teased each other all evening. "Come home with me, Darcy." He breathed into her neck, nipping her clavicle.

"I don't have a choice."

He pulled back. "Of course you do."

She crossed her forearms behind his neck, unable to stop herself from letting his hair sift between her fingers. "You live in my house."

"Oh." He nuzzled his nose against hers. "Come to my side. Stay with me tonight."

"All night?"

"I'm going to need all night."

She shivered. He wasn't being boastful. She could see it in his eyes—he was going to take his time. She wanted him. She couldn't deny it, not when she'd been a live wire of sensations since that moment under the tree. This was her last night to do something for herself. She'd have to face Mr. and Mrs. Blackstone tomorrow. And her Thanksgiving wouldn't be her own. She would need to be at the store at three the day after to ready it for the five a.m. door busters.

She nodded. It would need to last her for a while.

She couldn't wait any longer. The rules didn't apply to anything that had Ben in the subject line. And she liked it that way.

SEVEN

His headlights cut through the deep blackness of their neighborhood. At two in the morning there was barely a light on. The streetlamps were on sensors, clicking on as they drove past the stone sign for Oakwood Gardens, like a halogen arrow leading them home.

He parked his truck on his side of the driveway. Darcy pulled in after him, her coupe silent on the recently sealed blacktop. He stepped down, his work boots crunching on the frosted lawn. His breath curled in front of him, a wispy specter of heat on the cold night.

The little tree was a spotlight, a mini-me to the tree they'd worked on all night. Twin spheres of light above each of their doors was a final bit of welcome. The winter white of her coat emphasized the paleness of her cheeks. Her fair hair that wouldn't stay in its bonds made his fingertips itch to get into all of that silk. But it was the dark watchfulness of her eyes that was his undoing. They didn't rush. Instead, they climbed the stairs together. Her pinkie brushed his forefinger, but that was their only contact.

He dug out his keys and opened the door, backing his way in. She passed him, the whisper of wool brushing against his own peacoat.

He shut the door and followed, clicking on a light. Then he tossed his coat on a chair, curling his fingers into his palms. He was as eager as a teenager, for fuck's sake.

His hands shook a little as he came up behind her and smoothed his fingertips over the wool covering her shoulders. Her bag thudded to the floor. His knuckles grazed along her neck, the corn-silk softness of her hair tickling his wrists as he slowly drew her coat down her arms.

She looked over her shoulder, the dim light making her skin seem impossibly fragile. The freckles dusting her skin were even more pronounced. He placed her coat over the arm of the couch that bisected the room then came up behind her again. The curve of her bottom fit against his hips, her shoulders rested against his chest and the back of her neck slid into place along his. He circled her hips, his fingers tightening on the belt loops of her jeans as he finally took his first taste of her in his space.

He nosed his way along the endless line of her neck, trailing a soft kiss up to her ear. "This is what you want?"

She nodded. A small quake vibrated through her and into his chest. He twisted the denim and breathed through the urge to take. He wanted more than just clawing needs and recriminations in the morning. He'd had lifetimes of that. This woman was more than mistakes and misdeeds.

He smoothed his palm over her midriff, lifting her shirt until he found skin. She covered his hand with her own, bringing him up to cup her breast. The simple cotton burned under his palm. Or was it the bead of her nipple against the heel of his hand? She slowly swayed against him. The curve of her bottom brushed against his jeans and a little hiccupping sigh melted into him.

With his other hand he dipped down over her jeans and guided her closer. The tips of his fingers hovered over the seam of her jeans, his palm cupping and squeezing her breast as he kissed her neck. She heated under his touch like a slow candle flame that could, and probably would, burn him alive.

Tucking into the natural curve of her, he hardened against the cleft of her bottom. He unzipped her jeans, all the while teasing one nipple, then the other, through the lightweight cotton. His tugs grew sharper with each bite of her nails into his wrist as she clung to his forearm.

He drew the fleshy lobe of her ear between his teeth, the wild ocean scent of her strongest behind her ears. Her hair was full of the clean scent. It seemed fitting since the damn ocean seemed to be roaring between his ears. He dipped his fingers down into her jeans, finding more cotton and then soft, slick flesh. He groaned against her neck and pushed lower.

She rolled her head against his collarbone, her hips jerking under his touch. He held her tighter. His dick was near strangled in his jeans, but he wouldn't stop even if his damn house was on fire. No, her house was on fire. His rhythm stuttered for a moment and he put that thought out of his mind, concentrating on her pleasure, on feeding the hunger within him into her. He wanted to hear her cry out his name. Wanted to know it was him that made her feel like this and not just a willing body.

He loved that he could bring out her laughter and her passion. He hooked the tips of two fingers deeper. Slick with her excitement, he pressed harder until the friction of his fingers made her gasp and twist against him. Her nails scraped down his arm, through the hair. "You feel so good. Hot and wet."

She whimpered and the shudder that racked her made him ache to be inside her. To feel that clench around him. She drew her other hand up to his hair and held him tighter to her even as they both bowed under the strength of her release.

"That's it, darlin'. Let go. God, you're so fucking beautiful."

And she was. Sweet and so goddamn responsive. She twisted in his arms, wrapping around him as she buried her face in his neck. He gripped her hips, banding his forearms around her waist. Stunned, he held her firm. "Hey, it's okay."

She shook her head and the sniffle of emotion surprised him. "I'm sorry."

He buried his hands in her hair and pressed her cheek to his chest. "Don't be sorry. You're beautiful. That was beautiful."

"I feel stupid."

He leaned back, drawing her chin up. The wetness on her cheeks humbled him. This woman was so wrapped into herself, so tightly controlled, hadn't she ever just let go? "Don't. You're anything but stupid." He leaned down, pressing his mouth to hers. "Come upstairs with me."

She ducked her head, then lifted her gaze to his and nodded.

With linked fingers they climbed the steps. At the top, she pulled to the left but he shook his head. "This way." He drew her down the dark hallway. A tiny LED nightlight glowed from his bathroom. When he flicked the light switch inside his bedroom door, a small desk lamp lit the corner, leaving them in muted shadow. He stopped in the middle of the room, his king-sized bed at her back. He pushed her hair over her shoulder and followed the curving line of her t-shirt that dipped just below her clavicle. He trailed the tips of his fingers over her curves until he found the bottom of her shirt and lifted it.

She raised her arms, goose bumps flooding down and her nipples tightening against the smooth cotton of her simple white bra. He reached behind her, carefully unhooking it, and drew the straps down. Trying to take things slow, he took a deep breath. Her nipples were a few shades darker than the freckles that dusted her entire upper half. He cupped the pale weight of her breasts, brushing his thumbs lightly over her tight peaks.

Her eyes fluttered shut and her lips parted as he plucked the tips.

Going slow might just kill him.

But he was more than willing to throw himself into the fray if it extended the night.

He trailed lightly over her ribs and dragged her in, lifting her into his arms. She gasped and grabbed hold of his shoulders, hooking her ankles at his back.

He latched his mouth to her throat and a low groan escaped. "You have the longest goddamn legs. I'm going to lay you out and taste every inch before tonight is over."

She slipped her hands into his hair and drew his mouth to hers. The kiss was hot and anything but slow. He tumbled them onto his bed. Her quick laugh made his dick even harder as she propped herself up on her elbows and looked at him.

He knelt between her thighs. "What?"

"I did not expect to do this tonight." She tugged at his shirt until it came up over his head. He smiled down at her. Pale hair tumbled over his midnight-colored sheets. She smoothed her palm over his shoulders, down his arm that wasn't inked and pulled his hand up to her face. Peach-soft skin filled his palm, demanding patience where he wanted only to take. She explored her way down his other arm, smoothing the pad of her thumb over the flames that exploded around his shoulder and down to the flashpoint where the tree sat, then down the serpentine body of the dragon that hugged his forearm. The tip of her nail traced the dragon tail that circled his wrist, the point accentuating the Chinese character that bloomed over the inside of his wrist in a deep red.

"What does this mean?"

"Hope."

She looked up at him and drew her hands up to cup his face, pulling him down on top of her. The first contact of his skin to hers was so good he hissed out a groan. The tips of her breasts burned into his skin. She opened her legs, cradling him into her. He dug his knuckles into the mattress and lifted himself over her, undulating his hips against where his body wanted to go most.

She gripped his back, her fingertips tightening on his lower spine to draw him closer. Her deep green eyes were wide and so fucking innocent it made his chest ache. She trailed her nails around his belly. The tickle had him arching over her.

Then she levered herself up and flipped him, straddling his thighs with a wide smile. Her long, graceful fingers went to his belt.

"The slow thing? Maybe when I'm not so wound up I could scream I'd appreciate it. But right now?" She flicked her tongue around his navel. "Can't wait."

His cock was pulsing with each pull of her fingers at his fly. His belly tightened as her cool fingers slid under the band of his boxers. He lifted his hips, groaning as she reached around and dragged his jeans and boxers down over his ass. She crawled backward and the tip of his cock grazed her cheek.

Fuck.

He was the one on his elbows now, staring down at her. The mass of her silky straight hair slid over her shoulder and tickled his thighs. "Christ, Darcy."

Suddenly she turned around, straddling his thighs, facing his feet. She grinned over her shoulder. "Laces."

He dropped back and threw an arm over his eyes. His cock was so fucking hard it pressed against his belly at an angle. He lifted his arm and peeked, groaning as her ass wiggled in her loosened jeans while she went at his double knots. He tried to move, tried to toe them off, but her hands braceleted his ankles.

"Patience."

"Didn't you just say you were done with the slow thing?"

"You playing it slow yes, me?" She flicked a smile at him. "I didn't say anything about me taking my time."

"I'm staring at your ass, and if you don't finish with those laces I'm going to drag off your jeans and show you just why that position is a dangerous one."

She rose onto her knees and he felt the coolness on his feet. He kicked off his jeans, slid his legs out from under her and gripped her hips. Instead of turning around, she pushed her jeans over her hips. "Why so dangerous, Ben?" The pink of her panties had a dark spot from how wet he'd gotten her downstairs. Trapped at her knees, her jeans wouldn't go any farther unless she got off him. And that just wasn't fucking happening.

He pushed aside the elastic leg and touched her. She gasped and stilled. Not enough, not nearly enough. He dragged her panties down and swore. Her pussy was wet and perfect and so goddamn tempting he wasn't sure he could keep himself in check. The slope of her back, the dimples at each side, so many freckles he could spend a lifetime counting them.

"Darcy."

She looked over her shoulder, her eyelids heavy and the green nearly obliterated by her pupils. Decision made, he reached back for his nightstand and found a condom. He slid his fingertips down her spine, ticking over each vertebra until her hips filled his palms. She arched under his touch, lifting herself to him.

Darcy's thighs tingled and her breasts ached so much she had no choice but to cup them for relief. He tugged off her jeans. Never had she felt so overwhelmed within her own skin. It was as if he could reach inside her and manipulate every emotion, every trigger. And here, now—with herself on display for him—all she could concentrate on was him filling her. Filling her more than anyone else ever had.

She'd thought that this position would lessen the intimacy, break some of the stranglehold he seemed to have on her, but it was worse. So much worse. The heat of him behind her sucked the air out of her lungs. The rough hair of his thighs, the firm grip of his hands on her hips, the way he seemed to fill the room until all she could focus on was him.

She felt the blunt end of him against her.

Oh God.

He curled over her and slowly sank into her. Her thighs quaked and her wrists shook. He was everywhere. All around her and pushing out from within her. His arms curled around her belly and up to cup her breasts as he stayed there. So full she couldn't take a breath. He tucked his chin into her neck and his shallow breaths matched her own as he slid out and back inside on a deep groan.

He stretched her up until only her knees supported her. She widened her stance and reached back for balance, gripping his neck, his hair—anything not to fall forward. Her back arched to accommodate the new position and keep him inside her. She felt displayed to the room. She opened her eyes and saw the mirror.

"Ben."

His name was devoid of air. Instead her voice was only need. He was behind her, his dark eyes blazing with something she'd never seen before. She watched as his hands cupped her, tugging at her nipples lightly as he slowly pulsed inside her. Each thrust was shallow. As if he couldn't bear to be away from her skin.

She lifted both arms over her head, his feathery soft hair sifting through her fingers. He invaded every one of her senses. Finally one hand traced down her ribs to the soft curve of her belly.

He scraped his teeth along her neck. The edge of his thumbnail rimmed her bellybutton. "I'm going to make it my mission in life to taste every freckle on your body." His other hand lowered until both brushed the tops of her thighs and opened her even wider. She cried out.

It was too much.

The mirror angle wasn't quite right to see everything, but she could certainly feel him stretching her, her walls grasping to hold him inside. Suddenly he surged up, filling her until she was sure her body would split in two with the pleasure.

His hands slid into the vee of her thighs, the sides of his fingers opening her swollen lips until he found her clit. Part of her wished she could see. Wanted to know just how they fit together. Anything that felt this amazing had to be beautiful.

But she couldn't tear her gaze away from the mirror. She watched him watch them. And that made it all the more thrilling. They glided together again and again, the rhythm as enthralling as the way he stretched her.

"Darcy." His eyebrows knitted together as his thrusts became sharper.

Off balance, she pitched forward and her hips lifted. The sweet, fluid thrusts were gone and she cried out as he slammed into her. Her shoulders sank into the bed as he surged into her again and again. The sweaty rasp of the hair of his thighs against her smooth ones, the grip of his fingers on her hips, the abrasion of her nipples against the comforter with each thrust—all of it coalesced into sensory overload.

His thrusts were long and deep and hard and it was wonderful. She'd never been taken so completely.

He reached around her, his fingertips digging into her belly then finally between her legs. She could feel how close he was. Taste it in the air she breathed in so greedily. No one had ever wanted her this way.

He pulled her leg out and they slid forward in a heap. He must have come, because he stopped thrusting and fell forward with his full weight on her. She hadn't quite gotten there again, but that was fine. To be wanted like that was more than she'd ever had before.

But no, he pulled her leg out straight and rolled her to the left a little so she was pressing down on the knee tucked into her body. And then he was inside her again. The fullness multiplied. His long fingers slid down inside the seam where thigh met body and he rubbed tiny circles around her clit.

She sucked in all the air in the room. And it still wasn't enough. Her body trembled as he kept the constant circular pressure. The safe warmth was gone, leaving her raging inside. She searched out for something to grab, anything to hold on to. Fisting the blankets, she pushed back against him. Tears leaked from the corners of her eyes as she sobbed through the tearing release. His name was a keening cry ripped from her lungs.

His arms surrounded her, held her tight to his body as he drew her knee back up to match her other one. And still he didn't slide from her body. Surely she'd flown apart. He was just putting her back together. But no, he curled around her and thrust slowly. Sweat slicked between him and she felt his deep groan through her back as he held himself tightly inside her.

They lay like that for a long time, her breathing finally slowing until it matched his.

"I'm sorry, I have to move before we have ourselves a little problem."

She grinned into the mattress, laying her cheek against the cool comforter. She should probably stretch out, but she wanted to hold all of that inside her—hold it close inside the ball of bliss that she'd become.

There was a coolness against her back and the bed shifted. His weight was gone.

What was it about this man? This kind man with an equal measure of muscle and artistry that got inside her like no one else?

Had it really been only one day with him?

Gentle fingers coasted down her spine followed by a cool washcloth. "I thought you might like this."

Moaning, she slowly uncurled with each stroke of the cloth. She rolled to her side, wincing with each stretching muscle. Twenty hours at the store and the best sex she'd ever had was enough to slam the lid on feeling self-conscious.

She turned herself around and crawled to the top of the bed. Her body ached deliciously and she wanted nothing more than to fall on her face for ten straight hours. She tucked her cheek into his pillow and blinked sleepily up at him.

She should go home. It wouldn't be smart to stay. Things would get weird.

"Stay."

Her lips curled into a smile. "Reading my mind?"

"I want to hold you tonight." He leaned in, brushing a light kiss over her eyes, against her cheeks and finally her mouth. "Once isn't going to be enough, Darcy."

She opened her eyes. How the heck was she supposed to say no to that? She simply nodded.

"If you disappear in the morning, I'll find you."

The humming laugh surprised her. She should be annoyed at his directive, but she felt too good. "Because I'm so far away? That whole five hundred feet to my side of the house?"

His dark eyes were intense and for once humor was decidedly missing.

She propped herself up on her elbows. "I'm not going anywhere, Ben." She leaned into him, catching his lips in a soft kiss. Instead of the gentle Ben she was growing used to, she got another taste of the intense one.

Like the kiss behind the tree, he cupped her face and swallowed all of her doubts. There was no way she could leave this man and the feelings that swirled between them.

He rolled her back onto the bed, tightening his arms around her until there was no space between them. The lightness and the fun dissolved under his hungry mouth. The bone-deep exhaustion churned into a compulsion that couldn't be stopped.

This time there was no gentleness, no finesse, just a grappling urgency that they fed into each other. Soreness faded to the background as his lips coasted along her neck, across her shoulders and finally found her breast. She arched underneath him as he sucked her nipple into his mouth.

Her nails scraped through his hair, holding him tighter to her. He cupped both breasts, pushing them up for his mouth.

His gaze locked on her. The pads of his thumbs scraped across the tight peaks before his mouth returned with the added nip of teeth. She maneuvered her hand between them and cupped him. Her walls clenched at the weight of him in her hand, thick and hard. She swiped her thumb under the sensitive head.

He shuddered at her touch. "Harder," he said around her painfully hard nipple. He nipped at her until her grip firmed enough to satisfy him.

She pressed him against where she needed him most and the groan that erupted from him urged her on. She rubbed against his shaft, the ridges abrading her sensitive skin and the way he sucked on her breasts pushing her so close.

"Wait for me."

She arched under him, his name a litany as she rubbed her clit against the fullness at the base of his shaft. He cursed and reached for his side drawer, but she dragged him back.

"Don't you move," she growled.

The first spark of laughter returned to his brown eyes as he swiveled his hips above her, playing keep-away. She grabbed his hair, dragging him down to bite his lower lip. "You are a freaking tease."

He laughed, levering himself off her, and the snap of latex followed by a grunt from him made her feel better. Instead of crawling right back onto her, he rolled the tip of himself along her lips and under her hood.

"Now you want to go slow?" Her body was so revved she was sure she'd go insane.

"Can't you feel the anticipation?"

She dug her nails into his muscled butt and dragged him forward. They both groaned as he slid inside her. Her abused body screamed for him to go slow, but the clawing lust vetoed that idea. Nothing but all of his passion would do right now.

Everything about them together was so new to her. Sex was usually just something to endure for a little closeness and pleasure. But with Ben? No...with Ben nothing was simple. Her frustrated groan and hiss stopped him.

"Darcy?"

"Ben, please." She didn't know how to ask for it. She rolled her hips against him. Even as her muscles begged for a reprieve she had to get rid of this lightning ball of intensity bouncing inside her.

"Tell me," he said on a gasp as her muscles clenched down on him. "God, you feel so amazing. I want—" He cut himself off and stilled again. His eyes slammed shut as if he was trying to hold on.

She cupped his face. He had to feel the same. "I want it too. I need it, Ben. All of it."

He slammed into her and she cried out. He faltered until she screamed out a yes and then it was two people taking everything from each other. He dragged her knee up on his hip and went impossibly deeper.

His arms shook on either side of her head as he drove into her again and again. Sweat and the overwhelming slickness of her own body accepting him greedily turned their space into a sauna of lust.

She hooked her arms under his and held on to his shoulders as each thrust filled her with Ben. This wasn't just sex. This was them at their most elemental forms. When she came it was even more overwhelming than the first time.

She sobbed into his shoulder. It was just the only way for all the pressure and the pleasure to release from her. He buried his forehead into her shoulder as he panted against her. His body still sought refuge in hers. His thrusts grew into a madness that didn't seem to know how to blow itself out.

She clamped her legs around his hips and held on to him as they finally both broke into too many pieces to ever comprehend.

Darcy slid her fingers through his hair until she got to the top of his head and held on. She shuddered against him and dragged in embarrassingly huge gulps of air, but she couldn't let go of him.

He tunneled his arms under her shoulders and left himself pressed into her neck.

"God," she gasped. "Oh God."

"All the saints and angels heard us on that one, darlin'."

She laughed and flicked her tongue over the sweat-slick skin of his neck until she found his ear to bite.

"Hey, I've already been plenty abused here." She tightened her muscles around him and he hissed. "Dirty pool."

He was still inside her. Her body quaked with tiny aftershocks.

"Fuck, Darcy."

"It wasn't my fault this time." He shifted inside her and she groaned. "Not helping."

He nipped her shoulder and grinned down at her.

"You laugh, but I'm not going to be able to walk tomorrow. Hi, Mr. and Mrs. Blackstone, I had sex all night, but it's so nice to see you again. Let me hobble over to my section and show you how ready we are for Black Friday."

He dropped a kiss on her mouth, his dark eyes so full of happiness it stalled her breath. "All our neighbors certainly know, so they may as well too."

She groaned out a half laugh. "That's not funny."

Turning his lips into her neck, he kissed down to her shoulder. "I loved hearing you scream for me." He levered himself up on his forearms, his hips still pinning her to the bed.

He rotated once and her eyes popped open. "You are not..."

"What?" He looked down at her. "Not getting hard again?"

She could feel her face flaming. He was so open and sexual and she...well, she definitely wasn't. "Ben. I can't."

"God, you're adorable."

"Get off me."

He laughed and rolled off her, both of them groaning when their skin peeled apart. "Shower."

She threw her arm over her eyes. Exhaustion couldn't quite dispel the afterglow. Tomorrow would be soon enough to put herself back together. "That requires walking."

He hopped off the bed and she cracked an eye at him. "How can you be so energetic? You were dead just a minute ago."

"Sex energizes me."

She groaned and rolled onto her stomach. "This is never going to work out."

He popped her on the butt.

"Hey!"

"Sure it will. I'm more than willing to crawl right back into this bed with you after we have a shower. My energy only lasts about ten minutes."

She groaned. "No, you go."

He crouched in front of her. "Don't make me carry you."

"You wouldn't." She wasn't a tiny girl. The man was all talk.

He dragged her arm over his shoulder and hauled her forward, cupping his arm under knees.

"Ben!"

He swung her out of the bed and across the room before she could squeak out a protest. The fact that he didn't grunt or even stagger under her weight left her breathless all over again. He set her down next to his wide glass shower that mirrored hers. Being nearly six feet tall left baths out of her budget so she'd opted for ultra-large showers in her duplex plan.

He set the dials to a lukewarm spray and opened the door for her. "You look like the type that's going to hog the water."

She grinned up at him. She could keep this light. "Yep."

He leaned against the tiled wall and watched her under hooded eyes.

"You are not going to just stand there and watch me, are you?"

"Yep."

"Here, have some water." She moved aside to give him room.

He shook his head. "Suds and freckles are going to be my new favorite attractions in this shower."

She averted her gaze. He was talking as though he wanted it to be more than one night, but that was just silly. They lived on opposite schedules and had nothing in common. She quickly sudsed up a washcloth and tried not to think about how well they worked together or fit together.

"You're a million miles away."

Instead of answering, she put her face under the spray and scooped the hair out of her face. She jumped as his hands slid around her waist.

"We'll go slow."

She covered his hand with hers. "Nothing about this—" She closed her eyes because it felt too good when he touched her and swallowed back all the emotions she just couldn't deal with. All of them were too new, too much, and too mixed up with sex to comprehend yet. "Nothing about us has been slow."

He tucked his chin into her shoulder and held her tight. He seemed to know that now wasn't the time to talk about them. Instead he took her washcloth and soaped up her back and then her front, his hands achingly tender on her sore breasts and a little more firm on her shrieking back muscles.

How did he know her body so completely after just a few hours?

He crouched in front of her and she backed up. No, that was too intimate. She took the washcloth back from him. He brushed his nose along her belly. "I love that you smell like me."

She tipped her head back and closed her eyes. Gosh, everything about him was earthy and sexual and lacking in pretense. He gently nudged her legs apart and took the washcloth back. He washed her, tracing his thumb around the sensitive knot of muscles inside her.

"Ben."

"Shh." He washed the soap away and leaned into her and sipped.

Her hand slapped against the tile as he soothed her with his tongue and lips. Her release was so soft and sweet that she couldn't do anything but push his hair out of his eyes. His face was heavy with scruff and dotted with water, and his lips glossy with her. He stood, but before he could sluice the water and her release off, she pulled him down and tasted herself on his tongue.

He drew her back, his eyes already fired up. And again, she wanted to suffuse herself in all the energy that was Ben, but her body simply wasn't willing. She swayed a little and he kissed her forehead before drawing her under the spray again. They finished up, quietly drying off before they slipped back into his bed. Without words he settled her against him until his smooth chest was her pillow.

She'd never comfortably slept with a man before. She liked her space. But she slid her thigh over his and dropped off without another thought in her head.

EIGHT

BEN WATCHED THE SUN CREEP UP HIS MIDNIGHT-BLUE comforter. He'd forgotten to pull his blackout curtains before taking Darcy to his bed. Not that it would have mattered anyway. He'd been staring at the ceiling for the last hour.

Another day with four hours of sleep under his belt. He didn't care. Not when Darcy was curled so trustingly into his side. He slid his thumb over her shoulder and smoothed back down her arm.

He was used to sex being fun. He liked the feel of a woman in his arms. He was one of the few of his friends who actually didn't dread the morning after. All the other mornings were okay because it didn't matter if the woman was clingy or cranky or even indifferent. He could usually coax them into a good mood and they would leave with a smile, relationship or not.

But nothing about Darcy could be relegated into something so safe. The moment he'd touched her in the store he knew it was going to be different and still he'd wanted her in his bed.

His instincts never steered him wrong. From adjusting his major in college to leaving the safety of his job in Boston to start his own business with Cesar, and now the Christmas venture—all of it fit him.

But Darcy terrified him.

He'd known that opening himself up to her would be a gamble. And it still was. Hell, he only had half the cards in his hand and he was tempted to scoop up his chips and run. Except he wasn't going to run. He'd figure out some way to get to know her a little better. He really didn't want the cool Darcy back with morning-after weirdness.

The winter sun curled its fingers around her arm and teased the edges of her chin. Her lemon-blonde hair tangled across his chest. And she felt so good in his arms he was fairly sure sleep would be nonexistent without her.

When the sun crept up to her golden lashes they started to flutter. Her hand slid across his chest then down to his hip. He dragged air through his nose and didn't move. Morning wood took on a whole different meaning when a woman was involved.

She rubbed her nose into his chest and settled back into him. Her forearm skimmed under the sheet and her soft skin bumped the head of his cock. Her smooth thigh brushed along his as she slowly woke up.

Braced for the excuses, he caught her gaze flick to his nightstand. He didn't know what time it was, but instead of bounding out of his bed, she grazed her nose over his pec and swiped her tongue over his nipple, then dragged the back of her fingers down his cock.

He hissed when her swirling tongue was followed by a bite. He buried his hand in her hair, hoping it was enough to show her that he liked it. Her touch was tentative but his achingly stiff cock didn't care.

Hot breath blew over his nipple as she lifted her arm enough to see beneath the covers. Her name was a grumbled whisper as she stroked down his shaft and tightened at the base like he showed her the night before.

Efficient, that was his Darcy.

His? The possessive feelings from last night were already starting up again.

His hips flexed on the second trip up and back, his body tuned up from lying under her for hours. And he liked her weight. Soft and solid and long-limbed. Her kisses skimmed his ribs with open-mouthed nips and swipes of her warm tongue.

Silently she coasted over his belly, her cat-green eyes bright in the sun as she watched him. She dipped her tongue into his navel, pushing the sheets aside. He swallowed down the urge to paint her lips with the tip of his cock.

What the hell was wrong with him? He should be laughing and teasing her, using all his usual morning-after tricks to keep things light.

"I'm too sore for more than this."

He shook his head. "You don't need to—"

"It's been a long time, but I want to."

The tip of her pink tongue darted out, flicking under the sensitive dome of his cock. Again, her tentative nature showed, but the sun glowed around her light hair and her eyes were clear and determined.

He was a dead man.

She learned him. Slowly. His fingers dug into the mattress and he wouldn't be surprised to find chunks missing when she was done with him. She wrapped her lips around the base of his shaft and swirled her tongue along the throbbing vein, hardening him even more, paying attention only to the underside of him. The heat of her tongue and strong suction threatened to end it before he was ready. Christ, she hadn't even taken him all the way into her mouth yet.

She finally curved the flat of her tongue around his head and enveloped him in one hot, wet glide of her mouth.

"Shit."

She hummed around him with a wicked smile in her eyes, taking him deep. He brushed the tangle of her hair away from her face, not trusting himself to do any more than that. Everything inside him wanted to grab her hair and make her take him deeper. He arched off the bed as she finally found her rhythm.

Her nails scraped through the hair above his cock, splaying her fingers across his belly as she drove him crazy. He bumped the back of her throat and swore. "Darcy."

She shook her head, still working him to within an inch of sanity.

He grabbed her hair this time. "Darc." It was all he could make out. Her mouth sealed over his head, her tongue massaging the crown with each pull. And he was lost to the hot suction of her tireless mouth.

She looked up at him and he couldn't hold off any longer. With a muffled groan he came and she took every drop. Ben watched her throat work and his shaft disappear into her swollen mouth.

Chest heaving, he dragged her up until her nose was buried into his neck. He locked his arm around her, pressing a kiss to her temple. "Jesus, Darcy."

He could feel her smiling into his skin. "I thought a little payback was in order."

"Oh yeah?" He peered down at her, his chest tightening with the puffy state of her lips. All from him.

"Mm-hmm. Besides, watching you like that. All your muscles tight," she ran the backs of her fingers over his cheek, "and gosh, those eyes of yours."

"Do you really not swear?"

She wrinkled her nose and pushed away from him. "I just said all sorts of good stuff there, Hartley, and you focused on that?"

He laughed and hauled her back into his chest. *Lighten it up, asshole.* "Just an observation. I don't think I've ever heard anyone use gosh like you do."

She peered over his shoulder at his clock and settled back onto his chest. "My mother was so busy all the time with work and of course I was left to my own devices."

"So she dumped you in the Girl Scouts?"

Darcy poked him in the gut. "No. I lived in Boston."

"That should definitely make you swear."

"Exactly. I hung out with some rough kids. When I started

talking like them my mom proceeded to parrot back to me all the same things I'd said all night long until I couldn't stand to hear it."

He winced. "I'll try to curb the swearing."

"It doesn't bother me to hear others say it, but me? Yeah, she beat it out of me without laying a single hand on me." She snuggled into his side, her husky voice a rumble against his neck. "Then we figured out all sorts of dorky ways not to swear. Kinda became our thing."

He kissed her forehead. "Do you get to see your mom much?"

"No. She got married recently and her new husband likes to spoil her with cruises and trips."

He trailed the backs of his fingers down her spine then back up. She felt good against him. Her soft breasts and belly, her cheek back in its rightful place on his chest. "That's a good thing, right?"

"My mom deserves not to have to work every day."

He tucked her bangs away from her eyes. "Do you not like this guy?"

"What? No. Jerry's fine. Amazing actually."

"What about your dad?"

"He's not important." She slid away, dragging the sheet with her.

He rolled onto his side. "Darcy."

She flicked a glance over her shoulder. "I have to get ready for work."

He sighed and rolled back into the middle of his bed. It was a big day for her, but he didn't like the way she shut down. He had to remember they were still getting to know each other. He didn't talk about his own deadbeat dad, and she was probably the same.

She scooped her shirt off the floor. "Will you come in this afternoon?"

Lacing his fingers behind his head, he forced himself not to go to her. "Yeah, I have to go in and check on the shop, but I'll be in."

"They're coming at—"

"Yeah, darlin', one o'clock. I know."

She pulled her shirt down and let the sheet fall back on the bed.

"Right. I just wanted to make sure you remember. She wiggled into her jeans, stuffing her panties into her pocket.

He already missed the freckles.

She rushed out of the room, then back in and leaned down to press a quick kiss to his mouth. "I'll see you later."

He grinned. Not quite running. He'd take it.

NINE

DARCY TUGGED ON THE CUFFS OF HER BLOUSE. WHERE THE heck had she put her blazer? The Blackstones were in the store and she had Ben on standby in the break room in case there was a meltdown with the software. The lights had been on all day, but they hadn't turned on Ben's options yet.

They wanted to surprise the owners. Even though Miriam had told her not to come in before one, Darcy had walked through the door at ten. She had to make sure everything was ready in her department as well as the front displays.

"You are going to faint if you don't get yourself together."

Darcy laced her fingers together until her knuckles turned white. "Jaime, if I screw this up Miriam will have me back in the shoe department by nightfall."

"Come on, Darcy, everything looks amazing. You and Ben did an amazing job."

Darcy tried to block out the words *amazing* and *Ben*. Between the store and last night she was a wreck. "You don't understand." She shook out her rapidly numbing hands. "She told me this would pretty much make or break my chances of advancement."

"The Black Widow likes to instill fear in all who are under her. You're nothing but management in waiting. You know this store better than she does."

Darcy dragged in a steadying breath. "Thanks. I've just got to get through this reveal and to the other end of Black Friday and then I can breathe."

"That's a whole lot of days without oxygen, *mija*."

Jaime only fell into Spanish when she was worried about her. Darcy pasted on her best kick-butt smile and patted her friend's shoulder. "I've got to go get Ben just in case the tree shorts out or something."

The arches of her feet screamed and her dress pants pinched, the blouse was too big and the silky rayon kept untucking from her pants. She was so ready to hit the fire door and keep on walking. Gosh, she hated when the owners came in. She got to the break room and Ben was holding court. He had all the stock guys laughing as well as two cashiers on break completely enthralled.

She did not need his charm. Not right now.

He looked up and the quick half grin liquefied her knees. It was the same grin he'd given her in the shower when he'd been kneeling in front of her. And that thought needed to be banished. Now.

"If you're done entertaining?"

His eyebrow rose and he pitched his empty soda bottle into the recycling bin. "All right, guys, I gotta go earn my keep."

Her shoulders tightened. Again, she was reminded of the favor she owed him. She hated to be indebted to anyone. But it would be worth it if she could just get through this day. She backed out the door and into the blessedly empty hallway. "Okay, I just— What are you doing?"

He crowded her, his thighs pinning her to cool wall. "You need to relax and I know just the thing."

She slapped her hands on his chest. "This is not the thing!" She looked down the hall. He dipped his head and she gripped his chin, turning his head before their lips could connect.

"Hey!"

"This is not the time, Ben," she whispered. "My bosses are here."

"Yeah, and you need to relax. They're just people."

"They are not just people. This is my butt on the line."

"They aren't any better than you or me."

"I didn't say that."

"You didn't have to. Look, Darc, this is no big deal. We tested the lights last night and again when I came in a little while ago. They work and they look great."

"It has to look great."

"It will." He laid his hands on her shoulders. "Hey, they're going to love it and you'll be employee of the century."

"Ben."

"Don't get that school librarian voice on. I told you I'd get you out of this jam and I did."

"I still can't believe you came in and did it all."

"Yeah, well, it's the least I could do."

She frowned. "What do you mean, least you could do?"

He looked down at his shoes. "This is helping me out just as much, remember?"

"Right." She shook her head. The quick flash of something in his eyes didn't sit right with her, but she had too much to deal with to worry about Ben today.

He walked ahead of her and turned back to her. "Shake a tail feather, darlin'. We got a kick-ass display to show off."

"I'll catch up." She couldn't stop her lips from twitching into a smile. And all of a sudden she noticed that he had black slacks on, as well as dress shoes and a deep burgundy dress shirt. He'd spent the time to dress up for her, to hide the tats on his arms and to make a good impression. And she was being a prudish brat.

She'd been off balance since he'd started in on the personal post-coital talk and now she was making everything awful. And showing just what an uptight idiot she was about this possible promotion.

"Son of a beach ball."

"Ms. Tucker?"

Darcy's spine snapped straight. Miriam's disapproving voice was enough to push thoughts of Ben to the back of her mind. "I just sent Mr. Hartley up to check on the display before we met with your parents."

"Excellent. I trust there aren't any problems?" In other words, her butt was in a sling if there were.

"Absolutely not. We've tested it twice. I think they're going to be very pleased."

"I think you're correct."

She turned to go and Miriam touched her arm.

"Darcy." Miriam twisted the slim signet ring on her right hand until it was perfectly centered. "I know I've put a lot of pressure on you, but there's a reason for that."

"Oh?"

"My parents haven't made the announcement yet, but they're opening a store in Boston and they want me to go and oversee it."

"Wow." Her heart began to pound in her ears. What did that mean? They'd have to break in a new store manager? She'd just gotten so she knew what to expect with her job and a new boss would change everything.

"They want—no, I want—my replacement to be you."

The roaring in her head faded as if she'd been shoved into a vacuum. "I'm sorry?"

"It's going to be a few months before the store will be ready for me to go and open so we'll have time to train you properly. I need to be sure this store will be in good hands. And I think those hands are yours."

"I-I don't know what to say."

"You stepped up with this Christmas tree debacle and you're obviously a problem solver. I wish it had been a bit cheaper on the budget, but I think the new design makes us look even classier and I have a feeling it will translate into sales. And your Mr. Hartley certainly has himself a job when the Boston store opens. And he'll be paid handsomely this time."

"I'll tell him. This is a prototype. It will certainly put him on the map."

"And you said he's an artist?"

She nodded. Ben was going to be ecstatic. This design was his baby. He wouldn't just be a tattoo artist anymore. He could sell the design and do anything he wanted.

"Well, I'm happy to see him in more business-minded clothing today. I appreciate that."

A little niggling of unease fluttered under her breastbone. "I think Ben—Mr. Hartley—understands how important this is."

"And the ghastly tattoos are covered. I was worried about my father seeing those."

"They—" Darcy wanted to shout at her just how beautiful they were. The meaning behind them was so obvious if Miriam had taken the time to look at them closely. "He has a very good head on his shoulders," she said lamely.

"Let's go out and find my parents, shall we?"

Excitement pushed away any misgivings she had. She'd be running this store soon. She'd been preparing for years for this moment. And she had Ben to thank. She'd make sure she did so tonight.

Ben stalked to the front of the store. He was expecting her to be uptight—Darcy was uptight by nature. But he'd almost slipped and told her about John. He didn't even know if it had been his brother who took out the Christmas display, but he had a bad feeling. And his brother wasn't returning his texts.

And he didn't know—not for sure—he just wanted to bring a little hope, a little laughter into her pretty Christmas-colored eyes. He didn't even know why. Before yesterday she was less than a blip on his radar.

Now...

Now he didn't know what she was to him. He still wanted to coax a smile out of her, wanted to watch the slow bloom of pleasure take her over, and he wanted to hear her smart mouth.

Maybe he was being stupid about the whole damn thing. It was really extraordinary sex, but it was just sex. He had to remember that.

He ducked behind the customer service counter. Thank fuck Jaime was too busy with the madness that was Mr. and Mrs. Blackstone's visit to notice him. She was far too observant for her own good and he just didn't have it in him to make excuses right now.

He opened up his laptop and double-checked the code he'd hardwired into the music loop they ran every three hours. He ticked off a few extra songs to make sure they tripped the system while the owners were there.

O Holy Night came on and he rubbed his neck. The wonder and complete happiness in her eyes last night had been worth all the work. Knowing that his idea had worked so well was simply a bonus.

Darcy and her boss walked into the jewelry department. They were in deep conversation. Darcy was at her buttoned-up best. Her hair was trapped in a braid that didn't let a single strand loose around her face. She looked icy cool in her pearl-colored jacket and black pants. Her baby-blue blouse did nothing to dispel the untouchable aura around her.

He was fairly certain that no one in the store knew what burned under all that unflappable efficiency. She didn't look up at him once. All of her focus was on Miriam and whatever they were talking about.

"Stop snacking on her with your eyes, Benjamin."

His fingers flew over the keys. "Give me a break, Jaime."

"Yesterday I wasn't sure if you were good for her. Now I'm worried the reverse might be true."

His gaze shot to hers. "Why?"

"Darcy's got an innate ability to run this store."

He nodded. After just one day with her, he could agree with that statement. Multitasking and planning were second nature to her. "What does that have to do with me?"

"This store is her life. The only way she'd be more obsessed with it is if she actually owned it."

"I'm not a dumbshit Neanderthal that needs his woman's total focus, Jaime."

"Ah, but you're already thinking of her in terms of your woman. Darcy's not single because she's pining for the perfect man, she's single because this store is her man."

"A store isn't going to keep her warm at night."

"Maybe, but she keeps herself so busy she doesn't look at it that way."

Ben crossed his arms and leaned back on the counter. "Aren't you supposed to be the supportive best friend that gives me tips?"

She reached up and patted his cheek. "I am giving you a tip. You're a clever guy."

He frowned but didn't have more time to ask questions. Darcy waved to him. With a flick of two keys, he turned on the program. The lights hummed, brightened once and the trailing ants feature he'd added started at the registers and flowed to the podium, then spiraled its way up the tree in an explosion of twinkling lights.

Darcy's attention finally averted to his display. The quick and bright smile followed by more arm waving at him got him moving. The joy dimmed on her face as professionalism slammed down like a shield.

An older couple intercepted Darcy and Miriam. They were well into their sixties, with the stately demeanor of old money. Definitely the Blackstones. If the body language on the tall, white-haired gentleman and perfectly coiffed brunette didn't give it away, Darcy's sure did.

He slowed his pace, dipping his hands in his pockets. He was proud of his work, but he certainly wasn't going to come to heel for a bunch of blue bloods.

Miriam smiled. "Ah, there's our designer now. I was just telling my parents about your stunning lighting display."

Ben nodded and held out his hand to Mr. Blackstone. He was tall, but still a few inches shorter than himself. "Ben Hartley. I'm glad I could step in and help out."

He grasped Ben's hand in a firm shake. "From what Miriam tells me this was a mutually beneficial arrangement."

Ben smiled. The old man didn't like to be beholden any more than he did. "You were certainly the right test market for it, Mr. Blackstone. The original design was for household use, but I'm definitely open to modifying it for more commercial ideas now."

One fine white eyebrow rose. "Call me Max." He patted Ben's arm. "I'd like to hear more. The front of my store has never been more impressive. And that was even before the lightshow you've got here."

"Thanks, Max. I love Christmas. Working hard is worth the end product, especially when the kids come in to sit with Santa." He nodded to a little boy who had dragged his mother to the tree, already anxious to get into the huge chair.

"I agree. My Mary thinks I'm insane to bring in a Santa Claus so early, but I think it will be a welcome break for the mothers to stop in after they've done their shopping. And I've hired him on for every weekend until Christmas."

Darcy stiffened beside him and he had to force himself not to drag a smoothing hand down her back. The instinct was far harder to fight than it should have been. It would add another layer of chaos to her stressful schedule, but she'd cope. He'd only seen her in action for a couple of days and he was completely sure she'd figure it out.

"We'd like to discuss hiring you on for our new store in Boston next season, and of course having you come back next year. Perhaps with an even bigger display."

Ben tried to school his features but he couldn't quite cover the shock. Another store? "Yes, I'd be willing to discuss that. Of course it would be a paid job."

Max laughed and slapped his arm. "Yes, you more than deserve payment. In fact, we've discussed a bonus for the above and beyond job you've done."

"No. I appreciate it, but this was a favor for a friend." He looked down at Darcy.

Darcy looked away briefly then bent her lips into a polite smile. But none of the sparkle was in her deep green eyes. "Ben is very generous. I'm just so glad that he could help out last minute."

"It really is the most beautiful thing I've ever seen," Mary Blackstone said quietly. "You'll be giving the Christmas windows in the city a run for their money, Ben."

"It was my very favorite thing about Christmas, Mrs. Blackstone. My mother and I used to take the train down every year before she died."

Darcy looked up him, surprise cracking her professional shell.

"Well, your mother would be very proud."

"I like to think so."

The soft instrumental song faded into *Ring My Bell* and the tree lights blinked and fired like fireworks. The bulbs that lined the trunk of the tree winked on and off, their disco-like qualities lending a fun edge to the overall classic design.

Miriam gave a delighted laugh that surprised all of them. She shrugged. "I love this song."

Darcy fussed with the cuffs of her blouse but her lips twitched. Maybe there was some hope for her yet.

TEN

DARCY PULLED INTO HER DRIVEWAY. EXHAUSTION SANK SO DEEP into her bones that she contemplated sleeping in her car. Too bad it was so cold. Flurries blustered around her vehicle as the last trace of daytime faded into night.

The visit had gone well. The front end and Ben's baby certainly put a good spin on the walk-through of the store. She hadn't been able to catch Ben before he'd left. He'd left a message with Jaime that he had to get back to his shop since Cesar had been alone for most of the day.

Ben had clients and appointments just like anyone else. There was no reason to get upset that he'd had to leave. He owned his own business and the fact that he'd dropped everything to help her was going above and beyond even for his Good Samaritan ways.

She trudged into the house and flicked on the news, curling into the corner of her favorite reading chair. When the weather came on with a report of no more than a dusting of snow, she let herself drift.

She woke to her television blinking, no signal up and down her screen. Her satellite had gone into energy-saving mode. She stretched with a wince. Four hours in her chair—not good. She spun her watch. Actually more like five.

With a yawn, she rose and checked her front window. Ben was home. She wanted to go talk to him about her day. She wasn't allowed to tell anyone about her promotion. Miriam wanted to talk to the employees about her leaving and that Darcy would be taking over as store manager. They both agreed that it would be better to wait until after Christmas to divulge that kind of news.

She took the stairs two at a time and took a quick shower, changing into her oldest and softest pair of jeans. Unsure of her steps, she put a cute bra on under a long-sleeved t-shirt. She wasn't sure if she'd be welcome at Ben's house, or if he'd even want to talk to her.

He'd been cordial with her, but Ben had a game face too. And she hadn't been able to read him during their meeting with the Blackstones. She quickly dried her hair and left it to fall down her back in a straight sheet.

One nice thing about Ben was that she felt comfortable around him without all her carefully chosen clothes and hairstyles. He didn't care about the professional Darcy. In fact, he seemed to take great pleasure in stripping professional Darcy down to her skin.

And she really liked that part.

Before she could lose her nerve, she grabbed a pair of diet sodas from her fridge and slipped outside through the back door. There wasn't any need to give the neighbors something to gossip about.

His house mirrored hers because of the duplex setup and the light was on in his kitchen. She climbed the three stairs to his back door. He sat at his table. A large sketchpad took up most of the table and a sweating beer sat at his elbow. Colored pencils and drafting markers littered the top of the surface. His long fingers moved quickly over the page before slowing.

She shook her head. Way to be a Peeping Tom. She knocked on the glass. He looked up with a smile. At least that was something. She smiled back and lifted her sodas. He opened the door.

Battered jeans with pen and marker drawings over every inch

hugged his incredibly solid frame. He didn't have on a shirt and the scrolling lettering of the tattoo along his ribs only emphasized his abdominal muscles.

"Hey," he said quietly.

"Hi."

"C'mon in, don't just stand there sawing off that pretty bottom lip."

Darcy stopped chewing on her lip. "I wasn't sure if it was okay to come over."

"Of course it is, why wouldn't it be?"

She set the bottles on the counter next to the fridge. "I don't know. The conversation in the hallway wasn't..."

"I was just hoping to make you smile. I should have thought about how it would look."

"I was just nervous about the Blackstones." Darcy crossed her arms, tucking her hands away before she trailed her fingers over his chest and down to the artistic lettering. Faith, hope and love—such a deep part of this man. Not even two full days in his company and she knew they were his trinity.

Everything about Ben was there for the world to see. No excuses.

"I'm sorry I had to leave before I could talk to you."

She rubbed her upper arms. His living room had been transformed into Christmas central. A huge tree sat beside the fireplace, this one a downplayed version of her store tree. But instead of the typical ball ornaments it was filled with handmade and individual pieces that obviously had been handed down through the years. "It's okay. You had to work too."

He stuffed his hands in his pockets. "I had to rearrange a few clients and Cesar was getting bitchy."

She frowned, meeting his gaze. "Was he okay with everything? I didn't really think about how much of an inconvenience it was for you." Darcy couldn't stop herself now. She stepped into him and slid her arms around his waist. "I'm sorry."

He rubbed his rough chin against her hair and leaned down until his nose slid behind the curtain of her hair. "Totally worth his tantrum."

"I'm glad." She rubbed her cheek along his until their lips lined up. He sighed into her mouth. The kiss was soft and easy. A hint of hoppy beer transferred to her tongue as they sank into the kiss. Already, he felt familiar and safe. Something she'd never thought to look for.

She drew her hands up the smooth skin of his back. The fluid bunch of muscles and Ben's raw energy emptied all the worries that had settled on her shoulders. She wanted to touch and to taste, to explore him like he'd done with her last night.

He drew her t-shirt over her head, dropping it onto the counter as he led her through the kitchen to the living room. She wrapped her arms around his shoulders and hooked her knees around his waist.

He boosted her up effortlessly. "You like to look down at me."

She laughed. "Not many people can lift me up like a toddler."

He squeezed her butt. "You definitely don't feel like a toddler."

She hugged her knees into his sides with a grin. "To the couch, muscle man."

He arched a brow at her. "You wouldn't be steering me like a horse, would you?"

"I've never been on a horse."

"Could have fooled me," he said, sitting down in the middle of his leather couch. "I was going to bring you upstairs, but if it's the couch you want..."

She maneuvered until one knee flanked each side of his thighs. "I want to make out on the couch."

He nipped her neck until her head tipped back. "Just make out?"

She delighted in the skin on skin, denim on denim tangle they were in. "We can start with making out."

He slipped his hands down the small gap at the back of her jeans and found the lacy bit of underwear she was wearing. "Man, I can't wait to get to third base so I can see these."

"Show me your first-base skills and maybe I'll let you steal third."

His long fingers slid into her hair, drawing her face to his. Instead of the hard, hot kiss she was expecting, he slowed everything down. Lips barely brushed hers before they were gone to whisper over her eyes and cheeks.

Her whole body hummed at the gentle coaxing. She'd wanted to do the exploring, but how was she supposed to keep to her own plan when he touched her like this? Gentle Ben was going to be the death of her.

The clasp of her bra loosened. "I think I'm going to steal second base instead," he said against her throat. She smiled, but instead of a laugh it slid into a low, slow groan. His tongue swirled around her nipple before sucking, only to repeat the steps again and again until every nerve ending throbbed. She held him tight to her as she slowly rocked against him. The overwhelming feelings he stirred in her prickled at the edges of her consciousness.

Ben didn't know how to do anything in half measures. He cupped her breasts, feasting on one then the other. He looked up at her, the tight tip of her nipple between his teeth. She arched back, unable to look at him. The intensity in his deep brown eyes was too much.

Every single time it felt as though he was staring right into her. As if he could see every darn thing. He was going to be disappointed. He was so open and giving. How could she ever be enough?

She slammed her emotions down.

No. This was just fun. They were new and shiny. All this was just new lust. It wasn't anything more than that. She rolled her hips until he groaned against her skin. "I'm not going to make it to third base, Ben. I want it all. Now." She rose onto her knees and struggled with his jeans.

His hips lifted to help her. "Fuck, where's my wallet?"

She opened her eyes, her chest heaving. He caught her nipple in his mouth again, this time a little of the patient Ben missing. He nipped at her skin and she shuddered over him. She looked around again and spotted the battered billfold on the coffee table behind her.

"Hold me."

"What?" His head came up and his fingers wrapped around her waist. "Hold? Fuck me, Darcy."

She arched back and snagged his wallet, then handed it back to him with a smile. "I was really good at gymnastics."

"I'm going to remember that," he said, flicking out a condom. He covered her mouth, his tongue slipping out to tease as he laughed. "Holy shit, am I going to remember that."

She stood and wiggled out of her jeans. He stopped her, tracing his thumb over the scalloped edges of her cotton candy-pink lace thong. "Women's undergarments were created to kill men."

"They sure weren't created for our comfort." She laughed. The cute panties landed in the pile of her clothes. She toed off her slip-ons and climbed back onto him. "Now, where were we?"

He cupped his hands around his mouth and made a crowd roaring sound. She giggled and stole the condom. "Home run indeed." She peeled back his jeans and sighed. He was beautiful. She lightly grazed the underside of his head with her knuckle. He hissed and she gripped him firmly.

He pushed up into her hand, the low growl returning. Everything about him was so muscled and smooth, even this part of him that made her feel so sexy and powerful. She covered him first with latex and then sheathed him with herself.

Slowly, oh so slowly, she took all of him until there was only them meeting in every way. She cupped his face, watching his eyes as she slowly rose and fell over him. His jaw clenched and a muscle flexed in his cheek as she swirled her hips in time with each clasping stroke.

She tried to focus on how he felt instead of the tears that wanted to spiral up and take over each time he touched her. He gripped her hips, guiding her for a deeper thrust. Her head tipped back as pleasure crept in.

Instinct and desire took over as sweat slid down her spine and between them. It only added to the excitement, the scent of them and the way she softened to take him deeper. She shouted out his name, shuddering and shaking around him as he pulled her in. One arm came up her back, anchoring her to him until their mouths slanted against each other.

She wrapped her arms around him. They were a tangle of sweat and arms and her nose was buried in his neck. Somehow she held on to the sobs and simply quaked in his arms.

Always too much.

She didn't understand why it had to be so overwhelming each time. She couldn't breathe around the need and the emotions he pulled out of her so effortlessly. She laid her head on his shoulder, willing herself to calm.

"Darcy, sweetheart, I have to move."

She leaned back. "Sorry."

He cupped her cheek, drawing her gaze to his face. "Well, you know that silly thing about condoms."

She smiled because she knew she was supposed to. Now she felt weird again. He was so easy with himself and her and she felt as if every nerve inside her was jangling. She stood, slipping her clothes back on while he was in the bathroom.

He'd hiked his jeans back up but left them unbuttoned. He was smooth muscle and ink topped with that half grin. She sat on the couch. "Can you grab my shirt?"

He detoured into the kitchen, coming back with a fresh beer and a soda for her as well as her shirt. "Need some fluids?"

She huffed out a halfhearted laugh. "Thanks." She opened it and took a long drink.

He did the same and sat back, his feet sprawled out as he laced his fingers over his bottle. "How'd things go after I left?"

She tugged her shirt over her head and tucked her feet under herself as she nestled into the corner of his couch. "Really well." She relaxed. The store she understood. "That was why I came over here. I didn't mean to..."

"Use me for sex?"

"Ben!"

He laughed and tipped his beer up to his mouth. "You should see your face. Believe me, I don't mind. Use me and abuse me at will, darlin'."

"I came over here to tell you how impressed the Blackstones are with you."

"I kinda got that since they want me to do the new place."

"Yes, but what they didn't tell you is Max Blackstone is definitely talking about your light show. He'll be talking it up until you're chock full of new customers."

He sat up. "Yeah? That's great." He set his beer on the coffee table and turned toward her. "I'm glad I could help."

She frowned. "You don't seem too excited about it."

"Of course I am." He patted her knee. "I've been working on this for a long time. This was an awesome opportunity to try out my designs."

"Didn't you hear me? This could be a legitimate business."

His grin slowly faded. "I have a legitimate business."

"Oh, I know. But this could be huge."

He crossed his arms. "What exactly do you think I do?"

"You said you have a tattoo shop."

"Yeah, I have a business I run with my best friend, Cesar Luna. It's not a little hobby shop, Darcy."

"I didn't say that." She leaned forward. "I just mean you could make great money with this and have your designs in tons of homes."

"Money isn't everything. My art, that's what's important to me. I love Christmas so I wanted to make it fun and enchanting for families. Sure, it's a nice side benefit that I could use it for businesses, but that's not why I do this."

She tucked her hands in each opposite sleeve and put her feet down. This was good news. Important news that could help him succeed. "I didn't mean anything by it, Ben. I only—"

"I know. And for me I'm just glad to help someone out. Knowing that there will be kids sitting on Santa's lap and looking up at the dancing lights? That's the important part for me. The wonder is everything, Darcy. Do you even remember what it's like to just sit and enjoy something for the pure joy of it?"

She clutched both her wrists inside the tubes of her sleeves. "That's not fair."

"I'm asking a legitimate question. I know I don't know you very well—"

"No, you don't. I take pride in my work, in making that store as successful as I possibly can."

"That's wonderful, Darcy." His voice gentled. "But what do you love to do?"

"I—" She stopped. She loved her work. Loved her friends and finding new ways to make the store run smoother.

He moved to cup her cheek and she jerked back. He sighed and let his hand fall to his lap. "I'm sorry."

"For what? Obviously I'm the one that needs to be sorry. I'm sorry I don't have that pure selfless joy I can sprinkle around like pixie dust. I live in the real world where mortgages and taxes and people count on me."

His eyebrows snapped down. "Hey, just because I can see the joy in the holidays and want to create something to give pleasure, that doesn't mean I don't know about responsibilities."

"I've worked hard to get where I am."

"I know that, I can see that."

"I came over here to share my good news because I couldn't share it with anyone else."

"Why can't you share it with anyone else?"

She wrapped her arms around her middle. "Because all my friends are from work."

His dark eyes remained flat. "What about your mother?"

"She's on a cruise."

He pulled her hands away from her middle and gripped them. "All right, tell me."

She shook her head. "What, so you can just ridicule me about it?

I've worked my butt off at that place for twelve years. I deserve this promotion."

"I didn't mean it like that, Darcy. I just meant you only seem to work. I don't see you ever doing anything just for the fun of it."

"I like working." That store was her life. The people in it were her family. More so than anything else she'd had. "Miriam is going to run the new store in Boston. They want me to become store manager."

"That's great." He pulled her into his arms. "I'm happy you've achieved what you've worked for."

She pressed her cheek into his chest, closing her eyes when the palm of his hand smoothed down her hair. This was why Christmas lovers and grinches didn't mix. She knew he was happy for her, but he didn't understand her. "I'm going to be really busy. Miriam has to train me to take her place in just a few months." She knew the ins and outs of the store, but not the paper end. It was going to be a long process. An exciting one, but she'd be putting in even more hours than just the holiday rush kind.

His hand stilled in her hair. "Okay."

The tone of his voice was careful. She just needed to rip it off like a Band-Aid. The store was her life. She'd never make Ben happy. He was a dreamer, she was a realist. Didn't this just cement that?

She sat up. "I don't have time for, well...for this."

His dark eyes cooled. "Right."

She leaned forward, cupping his face in her hands. "You need someone who loves Christmas and has time for you."

He pulled out of her hold and stood. "You're not giving me the 'it's not you, it's me' speech, are you, darlin'?"

"No." She stood as well. "I'm just stating facts."

"No, you're running away before this gets interesting. If you wanted to make time to get to know me, to see if this went anywhere, you would. And I'm sorry for that. I haven't felt like this— Well, I've never felt like this about a woman."

Her stomach cramped and twisted. "Ben, I—"

"Hey, no." He held up his hand. "I might be a nice guy, but I do have a little pride, Darcy. If you want to walk, there's the door. It's your house."

She folded her arms. "I don't want this to be weird."

He laughed. A hollow, un-Ben sound. "We had a good time, right? A mutually satisfying fling. Tonight was just a nice footnote. I hope your promotion is everything you want it to be."

Her eyes hurt, they were so dry. "I couldn't have done any of this without you, Ben."

"Sure you would have. You're the most efficient and capable woman I've ever known, Darcy Tucker."

God, why did that sound so insulting?

She'd worked hard to be every single one of those things.

"I guess I should go."

Ben's usually warm and flirty voice was flat. Not cold, just absolutely flat. "Thanks for stopping by."

Thanks for the orgasm? She hurried to the front door and escaped to the porch. Resting her forehead on her own door, she turned the knob. Locked. "Just perfect," she whispered and trudged to the back of her house. The bitter wind made her eyes water. Of course it was the wind.

ELEVEN

BEN CLIMBED DOWN FROM THE LADDER, TUCKING THE LAST OF the clips in his pocket. He couldn't look at the house without wanting to hit his heavy bag every night. The only option was to take down the fucking lights.

She didn't want them up anyway.

And he was tired of thinking about her all goddamn night. His brand new king-sized bed was forever ruined by one night with Darcy. He could still smell her on his pillow. He'd changed the sheets almost a week ago and still, she was there.

He unplugged and tore at the painstaking swirls he'd made around each of the small hedges that lined the front of the house. He wound them around his arm. He'd take the materials over to his brother's house and set up a kickass display for Brittany.

That, at least, he could do. A few hours with his favorite kiddo would put him back to rights. He moved to the baby Japanese maple that sat in the center of her lawn. That one he'd leave. She'd have the little bit of decorations she needed to keep the Association off her back and still leave her to her Christmas-free world.

Perfect.

He threw the last bundle of lights and his ladder into the bed of his truck and headed out to his brother's place. John lived in a modest little house on the other side of town. The neighborhood was a bit more rundown, the yards a little spottier with crabgrass and dying winter landscapes. But the houses were still well-tended for the most part and it was safe for Brittany to play outside with her friends.

Ben pulled up and spotted Brittany sitting on the front stoop, the dull *thwack* of a tennis ball against brick never stopping. That wasn't good. Brit usually ran right over to him when he came to visit.

Her posture was stiff against the half wall of the brick surround porch. The right arm of her coat was pinned crookedly to her zipper to keep it out of the way. The white strap of an immobilizer showed against her neck.

"Hey, kiddo."

"Hey, Uncle Ben."

He squatted in front of her and tugged on the empty sleeve. "How's the mend going?"

She sighed. "I wish it would go faster. I still have to wait three whole weeks! I told Dad it doesn't even hurt anymore, but he won't let me take this stupid thing off." She shrugged and winced.

Sure it didn't hurt. He tugged on her messy pigtail. Brit had been doing her own hair since well before school, but it was obvious John was helping out. "Where's your dad?"

"Work."

He glanced at his watch. John usually came home before his daughter got out of school on the days she wasn't at the shop with him. "Is he running late?"

"He texted me. I told him it was okay."

"You have your key, right?"

She resumed bouncing. "Yeah, I was just bored. He gets mad when I bounce the ball in the house."

"Well, I thought I'd come over and decorate the outside. Want to help?"

Her huge brown eyes brightened, then dimmed. "How am I supposed to help with this stupid thing on?"

"You can feed the lights to me and tell me if they're crooked or not."

"So I get to tell you what to do?"

He laughed. "How did I know you'd be excited about that part?"

"I guess so." She stood, a quick flash of pain in her eyes before they cleared.

He pulled her in for a quick hug. His heart melted a little when she looped her arm around his waist and pressed her cheek into his side. "Everything okay, squirt?"

She shrugged her good shoulder. "Yeah. Dad just forgot about the science fair at school today."

Well, shit. Did he know about that? He'd hid himself at work for the last week. Cesar was going to take his half of the sign and run if he wasn't careful. He brushed wispy tufts of hair that had fallen from her ponytail out of her eyes. "I'm sorry, baby. Did you win?"

A dimple winked as she grinned. "Third place! Want to see my ribbon?"

"Absolutely. Go grab it and get me a Diet Coke while you're in there."

"Okay!" She ran off with the sudden exuberance that only came out of an eight-year-old.

He unloaded his truck and hooked the ladder over his shoulder. By the time she came back he was unwinding a double set of the fat, traditional lights.

"See, Uncle Ben!" She skipped across the yard with a huge foam board under her arm. Awkwardly, she flipped open the tri-fold project. And indeed there was a large blue ribbon tacked to the top corner. "This is Saturn."

He climbed back down the ladder and made the appropriate noises as she gave him an entire oral report about the planet from gasses to the rings. She'd drawn the planet, so this had to be something she'd worked on before the accident.

He took the board from her and oohed and ahhed about her ribbon until she was giggling. "Hey, why don't you go set this up on the dining room table so it's the first thing your dad sees when he gets home?"

"You think he'll want to see it?"

He pressed a kiss to the top of her head. He hated the doubt that crept into her voice. "Of course he will. And I bet we'll be able to convince him to order pizza tonight because he'll feel so bad."

"Pepperoni?"

"Is there any other kind?"

She raced back inside and Ben rubbed at the ache just above his eyes. He had to start paying attention to the people who were important in his life. Darcy didn't want to have anything to do with him and he had to remember that. When Brit returned, he smiled down at her and tossed down a little baggie of clips.

"Think you can give me one of those when I ask for it? And make sure the lights stay untangled?"

"Piece of pie."

He laughed. Neither one of them liked cake, so they renamed the saying. Kind of like Darcy did with her— Fucking hell. He turned to the roof edge and banished Darcy from his brain.

An hour later the sun was bleeding across the neighborhood full of ranch-style houses. He and Brit had the windows outlined in different colored strands and each square hedge decked out like ice cubes with rope lights.

The rumble of another truck dragged Ben's attention away from his niece. His brother stepped out of the tow truck from the garage he worked at. John's hangdog face had a few more lines under his eyes and he was sporting a calico beard. He shook his head. John never could grow a beard in one color.

"Hey, man," John said tiredly.

"Hi, Daddy." Brit fussed with her zipper.

"What, I don't get a hug hello, Britzilla?"

She forced a bright smile and hugged her father, pressing her cheek to John's solid midsection. John brushed his hand over her messy cap of hair. His tired face couldn't conceal the obvious love for his daughter.

"What have you guys been up to?"

She grinned up at him, both dimples denting her cheeks. "Uncle Ben-style Christmas of course!"

John pushed his ratty trucker cap off his head and scraped his mop of graying-brown hair out of his eyes. "Uncle Ben loves to run up my electricity bill."

Ben gritted his teeth, but kept a smile. "LED, old man. No more than a nightlight in the bathroom."

John grunted. "Well, come on in. Least we can do is get a pizza into you for your trouble."

Ben glanced down at Brit. "Want to go grab some menus? We'll be right behind you."

"There's coupons in the drawer."

"Got it!" Brit raced off, veering only slightly thanks to her rig.

John crushed his hat in his hands. "What brings you out?"

Ben shrugged. "I have late shift tonight. Figured I'd come and hang with Brit. Spread a little Christmas cheer."

His brother grunted. "Looks good." He zeroed in on the bushes. "Ice cubes?"

"Yep. We're going to put penguins on top when I come back. I bought them last year and stashed them in your garage."

"Good luck finding anything in there." John sighed. "Thanks for hanging with the kid. I got hung up."

"You missed a science fair."

"Ah, fuck."

Ben clamped a hand his shoulder. "Just tell her how awesome it is as soon as you walk inside. She's got it set up so it's the first thing you see."

John tipped his head back, his gaze focused on the sky. "I'm fucking up left and right lately."

"It's tough. But since Cindy left, you've been doing great." Ben shouldered him. "Might want to use the calendar app on your phone though."

John juggled his iPhone out of his pocket. "I don't even know how to use this thing except to snap a picture of kidzilla."

"Have Brit show you. She gets a kick out of being bossy."

"Christ, yeah, she does."

Ben grinned. "Hey, one more thing."

John turned around. "Yeah?"

"Tell me that wasn't you at Blackstone's."

John's brows beetled down and his brown eyes went flat. "I don't know what you're talking about."

Dammit. He could read his brother's tell every damn time. "Fuck, Johnnie. Really?"

John shook his head. "I don't know what got into me."

"Brit had her accident weeks ago. Why now?"

"I tripped over the bike in the fucking driveway. I don't even remember driving over to the store."

Ben sighed. "Yeah, well, the manager over there happens to be my landlady."

John's bloodshot eyes widened. "Are you shitting me?"

"I wish." Ben had gotten a rundown of the entire incident thanks to Jaime. "They called the cops."

"They haven't shown up." John's voice was belligerent.

"The last time you were in trouble you were what? Twenty? You don't look like you're twenty anymore. I doubt they'll figure it out. They weren't sure on the name."

"And you kept your fucking mouth closed?"

"Hey." Ben softened his sharp tone and took a deep breath. "No, I didn't say a word. I didn't know if it was you or not, but how many little girls have broken their clavicle in Easton? I was hoping I was wrong, man."

"What? So now you're going to go tattle on me?"

"No." Ben's gut tightened. He'd already fixed her store. She didn't need to know it was his brother. Not now. Hell, she didn't even want to see him, let alone talk to him. Not as if he gave her the chance. He'd been taking every late shift for the last week and a half. "I helped her out."

"Come again?"

Ben shrugged. "She saw what I did to her house and let me try out my motion lights on her store."

"Aw, crap. You're boning her."

"Shut your mouth, John. Don't talk about her like that." The anger was quick and he struck out before he could hold back.

"Shit, Ben. Didn't you learn with the last chick? Don't shit where you eat, or in your case, don't fuck where you live. Believe me, it's not worth it."

Ben knew John was bitter about his ex, but it wasn't like that with Darcy. "We hooked up, but it's no big deal."

"Yeah, if it wasn't a big deal you wouldn't be staring death daggers at me. Son of a bitch." John jammed his hat into his pants pocket, digging his fingers into his hair. "Look, just don't say anything, all right? I've got enough going on just to pay for those fucking doctors."

John made a good living as a mechanic. Just good enough to make them ineligible for the kids' programs for the state insurance healthcare. And the plan at the shop was shitty at best.

Ben sighed. "Look, it's a done deal. I rocked it out on her store."

John snorted. "And rocked out on the chick."

Ben winced. She wasn't just some chick. "Let's just get inside before Brit sneaks on the computer."

John looked at his watch. "She's gotta be hungry." And just like that, John went from angry shit to doting dad. His only saving grace was Brittany.

Ben ate with his family, letting Brit's infectious laughter choke the last of his anger out. By the time he'd downed a few slices it was time to head into the shop.

He had a few appointments to get through and a special request to go over with an eighteen-year-old kid. Steering people toward the right tattoo was as important as the final product.

He backed down the alley that butted against their shop and grabbed his sketchpad before getting out. He unlocked the tiny back door to his place that led to the storage-catch-all room. Cesar's playlist pulsed from every wall. He moved down the hall, flicking on the Tru-Lite overheads in his space on the lower level.

He walked out to the waiting room. A neon purple and red sign hung in the center of the deep plum feature wall of their shop. They'd designed the sign together so it had a bit of each of them. It had been Cesar's idea to send it out for neoning. He hadn't been sure about the idea until the sign had been delivered.

His best friend was very good at big elements of color. Luna Hart filled the center of the wall. Ben's designs were painstakingly lined up and matted on the left side and the right side looked like Gangland L.A. with Cesar's bold, bright style and haphazard mixed media display.

And just because Cesar was a crazy-ass idiot, he had a papier-mâché wreath hanging from the L in the sign. Instead of green and red, it was their colors.

Evidently it had been a slow night last night. When Cesar got bored, he started sculpting. The medium of the month was glue and paper. God help him. "Cee, where are you?" he shouted over the driving industrial music.

"I'm workin'! You know the music is only this loud if I'm mid-ink."

Ben climbed the three stairs to the upper studio where Cesar worked in a Plexiglas box. Personally, Ben didn't like the entire waiting room watching him like that.

Cesar was definitely the exhibitionist of their outfit. A woman with breasts the good Lord certainly hadn't given her was sprawled out on the extra-wide chair his partner had made himself. He was shading a delicate daisy around the woman's nipple.

"Uh—sorry."

"It's fine." The woman waved him in.

One of the things that continued to amaze him was the vast array of people that came in. Some were so modest he needed a penlight to do the work so they could remain covered, and some just didn't care in the least. Cesar got the ones that modesty forgot.

"I've got a few appointments, you?"

"Yeah, maybe four more today."

Ben nodded. "Cool, I'll catch you on the downtime." He went back out to the waiting room and busied himself with the day-to-day details that Cesar found too boring to deal with. The routine grounded him. Ordering in the special inks they needed for an expo, their standard colors, office supplies and cleaners. They couldn't trust anyone else but themselves when it came to keeping a clean shop.

The people in his business were fastidious for a reason and those that weren't didn't have any right to hold a tattoo gun. Disgusted that everything in his brain headed into negativity, he opened his sketchbook. That was one thing he and Cesar would always agree on. Sketch through the shitty days.

His evening picked up with a few walk-ins that he shared with Cesar. The newly of-age kid he'd been set to meet up with couldn't make it. Which was probably a good thing. He didn't have the patience to handhold and talk the kid out of getting a dinner-plate-sized skull on his back tonight.

He kneaded his fingertips into the tight muscles at the base of his neck and flipped to a fresh page in his notebook.

"You know, if you wanna talk about it or some shit, I can."

Ben looked up at Cesar. His friend rubbed at the severe fade that stacked up the back of his head. "Anyone as twisted up as you are has chick problems. I suck at chick problems, but I can—you know, listen."

He laughed for the first time in days. A week and a half without Darcy and he was a fucking head case. Cesar was so uncomfortable Ben was pretty sure the bottle of whiskey under the counter was going to come out next. When in doubt, get drunk. That was his friend's motto.

"I've been that bad?"

"Maybe."

Ben stood, slapped his friend's shoulder. "Thanks, Cee. I'm good. I thought I found someone, but it turned out to be a bit of a clusterfuck. Shit happens."

"Was she hot?" Cesar folded his arms over his massive chest.

"Yeah. She's that chilly kind of hot that warms up when she smiles."

"Tall?"

Ben frowned. "Yeah, actually. Almost six-feet tall. Why?"

"Hot chick at your six, bro."

Ben turned around. Darcy stood in the doorway of his shop. All the air in his lungs stalled, then backed up. He rubbed at the burning knot under his breastbone.

She had a blood-red hip-length coat on today. Her hair was windblown. Actually, a little on the wild side for Darcy. She stalked forward. "You took down the lights."

Ben lifted his chin. He didn't have to answer to her. "Yes, I did. You hate them."

She crossed her arms. "I told you to leave them."

"They're my lights. And I wanted to take them down."

The coat billowed behind her as she came down the three stairs to their lounge area. "You love those lights."

Ben stood his ground. "Not anymore."

"Why?"

Cesar grabbed his jacket. "Yeah, I think I'm just going to go."

Ben held up a hand. "No. Darcy was just leaving."

"No, Darcy's not leaving." She turned to his best friend. "Cesar, right?"

Cesar's eyebrows rose, the ring that pierced his right arch flipping up. "Yeah."

"I need to talk to Ben."

"This is my place, Darcy. You don't get to boss anyone around here."

She turned her attention back to Cesar. "Do you have more appointments?" That damn librarian voice came out, making his chest ache.

Cesar flipped his jacket over his shoulder. "No ma'am."

"Would it be too much of an imposition to ask you to leave us alone?"

Cesar smiled. "Man, you are so doomed. Just marry her and get it over with."

Ben tipped his head. Un-fucking-believable. "Traitor."

Cesar chuckled and clomped up the steps, his shit-kickers unbuckled as usual. "Doomed! I'm telling you right now, bro."

"Out!" they both yelled.

The door slammed on Cesar's exit.

"You can't come in here and act like this. You're the one that told me to take a hike. So I did. With my lights."

"Don't you think that's a little childish?"

Ben shook his head. "Practical. You should be proud, since you think I have too much fun to be serious."

"Don't give me that sarcastic crap, Ben Hartley. I came home tonight to a dark house. No warning, no explanations. Just—dark."

"I left the little tree lit up."

"Yeah, one tree, damn you. One stupid tree that looked so stupid and lonely in the middle of my dark lawn."

He cracked his thumb knuckle. "I should have left the porch light on. I'm sorry."

"That's not what I mean, you idiot." She pushed her hair out of the way. "Dammit. I've been getting used to the Ben Christmas that puked all over my house, and now you're going to take it all away?"

She was too much. Only this woman would equate Christmas with puke. "Tell me how you really feel, Darc."

"How I really feel?"

He folded his arms, digging his fingertips into his triceps. The woman was making him insane. "Yeah, actually. How you really feel."

She took off her gloves, jammed them in her pockets and grabbed his ears, dragging him down to her mouth. The kiss was imperfect and messy and she tasted of Diet Coke. He slid his hands under her coat and gripped the soft sweater she was wearing and held on, swallowing all the frustration she let loose and giving back some of his own.

She pressed her forehead to his jaw, dragged her lips over his neck. "I miss you, Ben. I miss your laughter, I miss your smell and I miss your stupid lights."

Dammit, she felt right in his arms. The weight of her, the way she fit, hell, even her snarky little digs at Christmas. He missed her. And now he even had pieces of her in his store. If she dropped him like a hot rock again, he was going to have to sell his freaking place. "I thought you didn't have time for me."

"I don't."

He took a step back.

She gripped his shoulders. "But I'll make time."

All the knots in his chest dissolved.

She hurried on, her evergreen eyes tired but shining. "It's going to be crazy until the season ends, but I-I need you."

"One second." He closed his eyes. He dragged in her ocean scent and shifted his painful erection in his pants. "Home?"

"Don't you have to work?"

"It's a Thursday night. No clients."

She sucked her bottom lip in, chewing until it was a bright raspberry color.

"Dammit, Darc."

She smiled. "Show me your chair?"

"My... Oh." He grinned, surprise and pleasure blending together. He twisted their fingers together, first drawing her up the steps to lock the door. But the light was out and the bolt was already thrown. Cesar was too smart for his own good some days.

He redirected them into his work station.

Her fingers tightened around his. "Oh wow." She looked around in wonder. One wall was an illustrated mural of all his original designs. He liked to test it out with airbrush before inking on someone. Each design was paneled like a comic book highlighting the best of the design.

She slipped off her coat and went right to the wall, her fingertips tracing over the curves of a mermaid he'd done for a famous model last year. "Did you do this on a woman?"

He came up behind her, drawing her back against his thighs. "Yes."

She looked over her shoulder, meeting his gaze, her mouth inches from his. "Where?"

"Her hip."

Her blonde lashes fluttered down so he couldn't see what was going on in her eyes. She was focused on his mouth. His dick tightened, strangling behind his zipper. "How long did it take?"

"Three sessions."

Her gaze lifted. "How long's a session?"

"For Amelia? It was three, four and two."

"Hours?"

His mouth tipped up. "Takes a long time to work on someone, darlin'."

"And you did it here?"

He shook his head. "When I worked in Boston. Though she did come in for a touchup a few months ago."

"How does anyone deal with that much pain?"

"For Amelia it was a lot of pain actually. The hip," he smoothed his hand over her corduroy pants, "is full of pain nerves. Even I haven't gotten one there." The velvety zip of the material under his palm kicked his texture lust into gear. He made a light circle on her hip and the side of her thigh.

"No." She swished her ass against his zipper. "I found all yours."

"Yes, you have."

"Do you get off on the pain?"

His Darcy was certainly curious tonight. "No. You get into a sort of zone when you're getting inked. Endorphins kick in and the pain sort of fades into a dull, hot ache."

She nibbled on her lip again. Her eyes were dilated with interest and curiosity. "Oh."

He drew the backs of his fingers up her ribs to tease just under her breast. "Do you want to get inked, Darcy?"

"I'm not sure."

His eyebrow lifted. "A virgin requires a lot of care."

"I'm no virgin, Hartley."

"Darlin', your skin is pure as a virgin's. Freckles over cream. You have to be sure. It's forever."

"Where does it hurt least?"

"Tattoos hurt, period."

She turned in his arms and lifted his shirt. His abs tightened as the cool air and her equally cool fingertips hit his skin. "I love your arm, but this..." She traced the trio of words that flowed together along his ribs. "I love this." Then she traced it with her tongue.

He groaned under her touch, his nipple tightening as her nose brushed under his pec.

"I want one here. But smaller."

"Are you sure?"

She nodded. A feisty grin slid across her full lips. "Do you want to pop my cherry, Ben?"

His cock throbbed. "Fuck, Darcy." How many women had said similar things to him over the years? Too many to count. But he'd never done more than laugh after his first few years as a shop rat for his mentor.

He wanted to mark her with his ink. More than he'd ever wanted anything in his life.

"You're the only one I would trust." She shimmied out of her sweater, leaving behind a lacy bra that had an extra panel of material between the cups.. Her toffee-colored nipples tented the cotton, showing through the lace.

"How the hell am I going to concentrate with you wearing that?"

She looked down. "It's just a cami-bra."

"Whatever it is," he ducked his head and sucked a wet spot around her nipple, "I like it."

She sifted her fingers through his hair. "You cut it."

"I looked like a boy band reject."

Darcy smiled down at him. "I like it." She scraped her nails through the messy short strands along the top. "A lot."

He stood up, drawing the tip of his finger around her nipple one last time before dropping his hand. "Do you really want to do this?"

She nodded. "Here." She moved down an inch from the bottom of her bra along her right side. "Hope."

"It will hurt there." He smoothed the pad of his thumb along the top of her rib. "It's close to bone."

"I broke my ankle once. Anything like that kind of pain?"

He smiled. "Not even close."

"I'll survive."

"Hop on the chair and lie on your side with your arm up over your head. There's a grip bar up there if you need to grab on to something. Your tattoo artist appreciates it if it's not his gun arm."

She nodded, sawing at her lower lip again. "Okay."

"You don't have to do this, Darcy."

"I know. I want to believe in hope again. Maybe if I see it on me every day I will."

He leaned down. "I'll make it beautiful."

"I know you will."

TWELVE

He moved to the thermostat and bumped the heat. She tried to calm the hummingbird that was currently trying to bust out of her chest. This wasn't what she'd intended to do when she got in her car.

The rage that had fueled her when she saw that lonely tree in the middle of her yard with the pathetic white lights had put her back into the car so fast she didn't even realize she was heading into the center of town. She had Ben's work address in her contacts on her phone and somehow she'd ended up on his street.

Every night she watched the driveway instead of the neighborhood view she loved so much. All she could do was wait for his truck at night. Some nights she woke to the rumble of his engine, some nights she even caught a glimpse of him.

Work was fine. She had a million things to do to distract herself, but at night?

She'd never ached for anyone in her life.

She hated it.

And she wanted to hate him, but one look at him and she realized just how stupid she was being. Every reason she'd come up with to cut him out of her life was as flimsy as wet tissue paper.

She slid onto the modified chair. Part of it reminded her of a dentist's chair with the hydraulics and cushioning. It smelled of lemons and the underlying burn of bleach. He took care of his studio.

No wonder he'd looked at her as if she was insane when she talked about replacing his work as an artist. Everything about the room screamed Ben. From the hauntingly beautiful artwork on the walls to the orderly work station, all of it mirrored the man she was just starting to know.

They'd rushed through the preliminaries and went right into intimacy. No wonder she couldn't find her footing. His Christmas designs were just an extension of the artist who was as at home here as he was in her duplex.

The same touches were in his half of the house. Orderliness with an overlay of art.

She lay back, stretching her back out to find a comfortable position. Ben was silently unwrapping new needles, which he deftly slid into a pen-shaped cylinder. He hooked the end in a small square contraption that looked like two spools. The quiet snap of a rubber band made her shut her eyes against watching anymore.

Not knowing was probably better for her.

"I'm going to draw out some lettering freehand and then transfer it on your skin, outline it and shade a little bit."

She nodded and took a steadying series of breaths.

"You don't have to do this, Darcy."

"I know. I want to." She really did. She trusted Ben on this. She saw his work on the boards in the heart of his waiting room. The colors were unbelievably rich, but the underlying art was what drew her. "Just keep it small."

When he didn't say anything, she opened her eyes to see him hunched over the table. His fingers were flying with a mechanical pencil, then he switched off to a marker. He was done with the design in less than five minutes.

"How's that?"

She sat up. The lettering was less than two inches wide in thin strokes of black and shades of gray. The E in hope tailed off into a star that wound into the center of the O.

"You drew that just now?"

He nodded. "Suits you."

She leaned forward and kissed him softly. "It's lovely."

His dark eyes gleamed and the smile rolled her heart in her chest until there was nothing but warmth. "Let me just go get it on transfer paper."

She lay back again and smoothed her palm against her jittering belly. She wasn't afraid of the word, no... It was the pain she wasn't so sure about. Surely it couldn't be that bad.

He came back in with a small piece of paper and snapped on black latex gloves. He rolled over to her. "Let's get you situated so I make sure this is good and straight."

"Where do you want me?"

He grinned down at her. "Flat on your back. Just so I can line it up."

She straightened in the seat and slowed her breathing.

He tapped and shifted the paper, taking a small spray bottle off his hip. "It will be—"

She drew in a sharp breath. "Cold?"

"Cold." His voice gentled. "You're doing just fine."

"You didn't even start with the ink yet."

He pressed down on the paper then slowly peeled it back. "Want to see how it looks first?"

She shook her head. "I want to see it when it's done."

"Your skin will be really angry and red."

"I want to see the finished product."

"Afraid you'll change your mind?"

She shook her head. "No, I won't."

He gave her a soft smile then rolled away to ready the rest of the tools of his trade. When he came back to her the gun had a small tube at the top. "The outlining really is the worst part. But I've been doing this for a long time, so I'll move as quickly as I can and then we'll see if you need a break, okay?"

She swallowed and nodded.

"Turn on your side. Good. Reach up and there you go." Her fingers wrapped around a grip that reminded her of a bicycle handle.

"Did you do this?"

"Sometimes all you need is something to hold on to. Makes it easier to stay still."

She nodded.

"I'll take care of you, Darcy."

She closed her eyes. "I know, Ben." The high-pitched buzz made her jump.

"Easy."

Easy for him to say. She held her breath, waiting for him to begin.

"Breathe."

She let out a slow breath and the tip of the needle struck. Her entire body stiffened and the quick shock of pain ratcheted up to a pressure-filled burn into her skin. She slowly relaxed as he fell into a rhythm of pressure, heat and the scrape of the needle then the swipe of cool cloth.

"You okay?"

She could hear the change in his voice. It almost sounded like his voice when he'd taken her in his living room that second time. Intense, gruff and focused. She shivered lightly and felt the hot flush of blood under her cheeks as her nipples tightened.

If he noticed, he didn't say anything.

He stretched her skin lightly and she could feel each curve of the O. She was expecting him to write on her skin, but the transfer seemed to become a form to him. The bottoms of the letters hurt the most, but that wasn't surprising since it was the curve of her rib cage. Just skin over bone.

Finally the pressure and burn were gone and the cool paper towel soothed her skin again and again. "I'm done with the outline. Just a little bit of shading and you'll be done."

The serious lines of his face melted into the friendly crinkles at the corners of his eyes. She could see why he had so many pictures of happy customers in the waiting room. Ben was easy with people and his calm nature put people at ease.

"Need a break?"

She shook her head, not quite able to articulate anything around the feelings that swamped her. He was a good, kind man and she'd almost thrown away any chance with him.

All because she was too stupid and afraid to see what was in front of her.

She sucked in a deep breath as the shading needles blazed over her skin. The sharp pain of the smaller needle had felt more like tearing. This was pure heat.

"Okay, lie still, baby."

She slowly eased back on the table, forcing her skin to press into the warm vinyl. The endorphins chased the heat and her nipples beaded again. It could have been a minute or ten minutes when he finally sat back, smoothing her skin a final time.

"You have such sensitive skin. It raised like crazy, but you barely bled."

"That's a good thing?"

He smiled. "Very good thing. Healing time will be quicker and less chance of scabbing over."

She wasn't sure what that meant, but she smiled. "Easy patient."

He smiled. And helped her sit up. The numbing heat faded, leaving behind what felt like a sunburn. He pulled her around to the floor-to-ceiling mirror that made up the corner of his room.

She gasped. He was right, her skin was an angry pink, but the shading was delicate and the star in the center of the O in hope was a soft, mossy green.

"I took a little liberty with the color for the star. I was going to stick with purple or blue, but the green reminds me of your eyes."

She lifted her arm and stepped closer. "It's... I didn't think it would be quite so beautiful." She winced and looked at him in the mirror. "That sounded bad."

He laughed. "No, I get it. You see ink on other people and sometimes it looks like it was done in a back alley."

She nodded. "Lots of basement tattoos happened when I was a kid."

"Cesar and I studied under different people, but one thing we both have in common is the art. His is a little more Miami and L.A. than mine, but we suit."

She turned to him. "Thank you. It's amazing. You must think I'm a complete jerk for saying you should give this up."

"Now that's a compliment, Darcy Tucker."

She rose on her toes and kissed him softly, grimacing when her skin pulled.

He laughed. "Let's get you lubed up and wrapped."

She sat on the table and he smeared a gob of triple antibiotic ointment on her skin and ripped off a piece of Saran Wrap. "Really?"

He laughed. "Best protection ever." He ripped off tape and stuck it to the edge of the table. "Now. I don't usually do this, but you're a special client."

Darcy grinned. "I bet you say that to all the girls."

He reached around her and undid the hooks of her bra.

Her eyes widened. "That better be just for me."

He laughed. "I can't say I haven't seen a lot of breasts and...other things in my career, but I don't ever touch the clients for anything other than the needlework."

The quick stab of jealousy surprised her. She'd never felt like that about someone in her life. Her number for relationships was laughable, but none of them had ever made her feel the least bit anxious.

He eased the straps down, gently spread a gauze pad over the wrap and taped it down. She nodded as he explained aftercare and keeping it clean, to ignore itching and keep it moisturized.

"Handy that I can give you some hands-on aftercare."

"Oh, you think so?"

He nodded sagely. "It's all about aftercare. And now that I don't have to play professional artist, I can taste these."

She let her head tip back as his hot breath hovered over her nipple before sucking one into his mouth.

"I watched them tighten when I was working on you."

She held his head to her chest, her grip tightening on his hair. "Yeah, I was kind of embarrassed."

He grinned up at her. "The endorphin high affects everyone differently."

"I'm not into pain."

He laughed and bit down, drawing her nipple away from her breast.

"Okay, maybe that part— Gosh, just like that."

"I'm probably the only man on this earth that gets hard when I hear that word out of your mouth."

She dragged her eyelids open. "What?"

He shook his head. "Never mind." He nipped her other breast, dragging the flat of his tongue over her nipple. "Do you want your shirt?"

She shook her head. "I want you to take yours off."

"Why, Darcy Tucker, are you going to violate my place of business?"

"If you have a condom I am."

He rolled back to his worktable, opened the drawer and flashed his wallet. "I just happen to have one on me."

"Very convenient." She tried not to think about him being with anyone else between the time they'd made love and today. Making sure to keep her smile bright when he rolled back to her, she reached for the condom.

He frowned. "Everything okay?"

"Good thing you don't have a parrot in here. You say that an awful lot."

Ben wrapped his hands around hers and stopped her from ripping it open. "Something happened between here and my desk."

"Nothing happened."

He dragged her to the edge of the chair. "You're the only person I want to be with, Darcy. If me saying something about other customers is bothering you..."

She shook her head. "I don't have any right to say anything if you did."

"Yes, you do."

She looked up at him. "I—"

"Darcy, when I'm with you I'm with you. No one else."

She nodded. Ben would definitely be true to any woman he was with. He wouldn't disrespect someone like that. That much she knew.

"Then what?"

"It's nothing."

His hold tightened. "Obviously not."

"It's just..." Her shoulders slumped. "It's too stupid to say out loud. I don't have any right to even ask."

He left the condom in her hand and cupped her face. "Ask."

"Why do you have one in your wallet?"

"One—oh." His serious face split into a grin. "I think I like jealous Darcy. You know, as long as you don't go all made-for-TV-movie psycho or anything."

"You're safe from the Lifetime movie original."

He laughed. "I took to having a few in my wallet when we were... Well, that morning after."

"Oh. Now I feel really dumb."

He tipped her head up and kissed her. "I like that you're territorial. It's hot."

She scrunched up her nose.

He laughed and kissed her deeper this time, then leaned back as she lifted his shirt over his head. She loved the wide expanse of his chest. He was hairless save for a trail of dark chocolate hair that fanned out below his navel. She swirled her tongue around the pectoral muscle, glorying in the way it tightened and rippled when she found his nipple.

His body was magnificent. She'd never been with anyone as strong and muscled as Ben. Most of the men she'd dated had been connected to the store. Either someone who worked there or was a vendor. But none of them were in Ben's league.

She splayed her fingers over his chest, flicking her thumbs under his nipples as she swirled her tongue over the striations of muscle that led to his collarbone. His throat worked and she chased his Adam's apple, nipping lightly.

"Your body is incredible."

His dark eyes deepened as his irises bled into his pupils.

She dipped her hands down over the ridges of his abdominal muscles to tease through the baby fine hair at his belly and into the coarse hair below his belt. She smiled when she got to his buckle. It was a wide copper fastener that mimicked the texture of a snakeskin.

Artist in every way, that was her Ben.

She unhooked it and dug into the gap in his jeans. There was a wet spot on his boxers and she groaned when she felt the pre-cum leaking from his cock. She peeled the material back.

It felt like a million years since he'd touched her. Filled her. And she ached to feel him fill her again.

His hands made quick work of her slim belt and she lifted to help him roll the corduroy pants past her hips. Her shoes *thunked* to the floor and her pants and underwear followed suit.

The material of his wide chair stuck to her as he pulled her forward. She opened willingly. He sheathed himself with the condom and tucked two fingers inside her. Her name was a soft curse as he tunneled deeper.

The curve of his fingers widened her, readied her and slid easily free. Whether it was endorphins or just being in the general vicinity of Ben, it didn't seem to matter. She wanted him and her body was more than willing to cooperate.

Another thing she wasn't used to. How was it that all it took was a look from him? She thought she was almost asexual before Ben. She never missed having a man in her life before. There was the store and there was her career. But now everything seemed to make less sense without Ben's laughter.

She hooked her knees around his hips and drew him in. "Just you, Ben."

He nodded and replaced his fingers with the blunt head of his shaft. His eyes seemed to grow ever deeper as he slid forward. Her lids wanted to close with each inch that he sank into her. But she forced herself to meet his gaze.

Fear clawed up her belly. Tears shimmered around the edges of her vision. He gripped her hips as he slowly rocked inside her. He looked down at them and so did she. Finally able to see how they fit. He disappeared inside her again and again. Her walls clutched and clasped at him. Every ridge and vein felt like he was marking her inside and out—making his place inside her body as well as her heart.

She wrapped her arms around his neck and her legs around his hips until no air could come between them. She felt a twinge of pain from her fresh tattoo, but she didn't let up on the pace or open acceptance of him inside her.

Her fingers tunneled through his hair to the top and his mouth latched on to hers as he swallowed her screams and the inevitable sobs that finally broke free. Locked around him, she tried to control the shudders. He only held on tighter and thrusted deeper inside her.

She heard the deep, guttural groan through her chest and into her mouth as he came. And in that one moment she wished for no barriers, even the condom to protect her. His name was a throaty moan as she finally let go.

THIRTEEN

BEN ROLLED ONTO HIS BELLY, BUT INSTEAD OF FINDING A WARM Darcy, he found cool sateen sheets. The last two weeks had been a series of juggling acts. Between Darcy's schedule and his own, they had barely enough energy to snuggle into bed together. Sometimes they came together in a fiery passion in the middle of the night, sometimes it was a sweet, whisper-filled dance of skin.

But it was just skin and light small talk.

They were too tired for anything more than that.

The college kids were home for break and today was the last day for Brit's class so he'd been doing double time on shop duty and Uncle Ben duty to keep the kiddo out of trouble. Today was the first day he and Darcy actually had off at the same time.

Which was why he was sleeping in her tiny queen-sized bed instead of dragging her over to his much more comfortable one last night. She'd promised him a little breakfast in bed and an entire day without plans.

He rolled onto his side, groaning at the clock. Six in the morning was only good for one thing—a long night of partying and going to bed when the sun was rising. He caught a flash of something in the hallway. He scooped up his jeans off the floor and half zipped them on his way through the door.

"I know, Jaime. Are you sure there's—? Right. No, don't call the Black Widow. No, I'll be there."

He crossed his arms with a sigh. There went their day off. She turned around and saw him, hunching up her shoulders. He knew it wasn't her fault. Being a manager in training, or even a head supervisor like she still was for Blackstone's meant that her time wasn't exactly her own.

Didn't make it suck any less.

She stuffed her phone in her robe pocket. "I'm sorry, Ben."

"It's okay." He opened his arms and she quickly moved into them. He rubbed his cheek against her hair. "Darcy emergency?"

"Tom called in sick."

"Is he really sick?"

"He better be," she said into his chest with a growl. "He better be on death's door, or at the least have the flu."

"It is going around."

"I know." She sagged against him. "And I certainly don't want him to drag that into the store and get every single one of my cashiers sick. Four days, just four more days."

He rubbed her back. "When do you need to go in?" He could feel her face scrunch up against his skin and he sucked back a sigh. "Now, huh?"

"I could make you breakfast."

He hooked his arms around her shoulders and pressed his forehead to hers. "Nah. I'll just head back to my house and go back to bed."

"You can sleep here."

He laughed. "My feet hang off your bed."

She laughed. "Do I need to buy a bigger bed?"

"Unless you want to keep sleeping in mine."

She kissed the center of his chest. "I do like yours."

"Good, then come to my place when you get out. I've got

Britzilla. Her dad has to work." As soon as it came out of his mouth, he wanted to drag the words back. What the hell was he thinking? When John picked up Brittany, Darcy would recognize his brother.

"Yeah? You're okay with me meeting some of your family?"

"Of course I am."

She peered up at him in the dim light of the hall. "Are you sure?"

"Of course. Just text me when you get close and we'll figure out dinner."

"What? You're not going to cook for me, Hartley?"

"Oh I can cook for you." He pushed her back through the door. He pushed the unease to the back of his mind and concentrated on getting her robe off. With barely any time to talk, he'd found absolutely no opportunity to bring up John.

How was he supposed to keep his brother away from the woman he was falling in love with? When she sighed into his mouth, he turned off the little voice and concentrated on one of his favorite things.

Morning Darcy.

They were a frenzy of skin and panting laughter. She was just as eager to get a taste of him. They'd both been looking forward to this day off. Darcy flipped him onto his back and a curtain of sea-scented hair fell around his face.

"Hurry," she said against his mouth.

He wiggled out of his jeans, kicking them and her sheets to the end of the bed. She knelt over him, her slim hand curling around the widest part of his cock. He groaned and pressed himself into her hand.

She slid the head of his dick along the seam of her pussy and he arched up, wanting inside her so bad, he sucked in a huge gulping breath when her heat surrounded him without a condom. "Darcy. Darcy, wait."

"It's okay. I'm on the Pill. And I haven't been with anyone in a long time before you."

He cupped her jaw even as she clamped around him like raw silk over heat. "Are you sure?" At her frown, he pulled her down. "I haven't been with anyone without a condom before you."

Her frown lifted. "I'm sure."

He surged inside her again and her slick walls grasped tight and hot. "You're going to ruin me for all other women."

She arched up above him and took him slowly. "That's the plan."

His fingers dug into her hips, his ink on her body stood out on her pale, pale skin. The pearly fingertips of morning curled around the edges of her curtains and then he knew nothing but the unending pleasure of her body welcoming him.

His fingers climbed up her back as he sat up and went ever deeper. He tangled in her hair and drew her head back. Feasting on her neck kept him from coming too fast. He wanted this to last.

The first time inside her with no barriers shouldn't be a quickie. He plunged inside her. Ocean-scented sex curled around them. Her fingernails bit into his shoulders as she rode him harder. The way she sobbed his name with the racking shudders that chased her orgasm kicked him into the beyond.

He poured himself inside her. The hot jets of his cum slickened her even more as he jerked her tight to him. When they both landed in a heap in the middle of her bed, they were fighting for breath.

"Holy hell."

He laughed. "Did you just swear?"

Her head came up off his chest. "Just what are you doing to me, Ben Hartley? Tattoos, swearing and more orgasms than I've had in my entire twenty-nine years—all within three weeks."

"Maybe the next word on my ribs should be debaucher."

She laughed and crawled up to kiss him. "Maybe." She groaned. "I want nothing more than to stay and do this five more times."

"Five?" He dragged a pillow over his face. "What do I look like?"

"Stud for hire?"

He reached for another pillow and whacked her with it. Her laughter made their ruined day off just a little less awful. He tucked his pillow back under his head. Maybe if he told her about John right now things would stay on a high note. "Darcy?"

She rolled off the side of the bed and reached for her robe. "Yeah?"

"Do you have to go right now?"

She leaned over him. "I need to beat Miriam to the store and make sure everything's good to go for the day."

"Right."

"Why? Is everything okay?"

"I need to talk to you about something. I was going to do it today."

"Well, that sounds ominous."

He rubbed his hands over his face. "Not exactly, but it's going to take more than the five minutes you have to take a shower."

"Tell me tonight."

He slumped back against the pillows. "Yeah, we'll talk about it tonight."

She sat back down on the bed. "Ben."

"No, it's not earth-shattering. And it's not about you and me. Not really."

"Jeez. That makes it sound even better."

He sat up and kissed her hard. "Nothing that would come between us."

She frowned and stood up. "Okay. If you're sure."

"I'm sure."

"Then cook me an awesome dinner and I'll forgive you anything."

If only it were that simple. He listened to her shower turn on and fell into a fitful sleep.

He woke to cold feet and an empty house. His six-foot-four-inch frame was not meant for a queen-sized bed. He threw on his clothes and headed downstairs. Darcy left a half pot of coffee behind, but it was stone cold and smelled old. He dumped the pot and rinsed it out, grabbing a soda from the fridge on his way out the back.

They weren't exactly hiding their relationship, but the mothers on the circle were too nosy for their own good. He had about an hour before he had to pick up Brittany. She had a half day, which put him firmly in Uncle Ben territory.

John had to work and he'd planned on spending the day with his two favorite girls. After a quick shower, he decided to grab lunch for the three of them and bring Brittany to the store. She'd get a kick out of the lights.

He parked across from the elementary school. Minivans, SUVs and station wagons lined the street. Buses dominated the parking lot and there were a staggering number of little people scattered everywhere.

They were experiencing a mild winter, leaving muddy slush and dirty snow as the dominant color of the landscape. He spotted Brit's bright-red scarf and cap and one arm in the throng of excited kids.

He'd be pretty excited if he had two weeks off too.

Brit carefully listened to the crossing guard and hurried over to him. "Hiya, Uncle Ben."

"Hiya, Britzilla. Ready to blow this pop stand?"

"More than. I have to read five books over vacation. My teacher sucks."

Being more of a doodler and sketcher than a reader, he sympathized. "Sorry, squirt."

"What are we going to do today?"

"I thought we'd stop by my girlfriend's work and see if you could meet her. And you could see the tree I did."

"The cool lights one?"

"That's the one."

"Excellent." She hopped into the cab of the truck and slid into the passenger seat. "You're not going to kiss and stuff, are you?"

He checked to make sure she was buckled in and started the engine. "I'm probably going to kiss her."

"On the mouth?"

Ben snorted. He liked kissing other things on Darcy, but figured it was safer to nod. "Probably."

"I don't know why anyone would want to swap spit. Seems gross."

He laughed. "I'll remind you of that when you like your first guy."

"Oh, I already like a boy. Max. He's really cute. But I don't want to lock lips with him. My friend Lucy said it's cold and wet and just," she shook her head, "yuck."

"I'm sure your dad will be happy to hear that you're not interested in kissing right now."

"Knowing Dad, he'd find Max and break him over his knee like in a wrestling move that Kane does."

"You guys still watch that stuff?"

She shrugged. "Yeah, Dad likes it."

Ben had never gotten into wrestling. Of course he'd been the odd man out with markers while John was taking apart everything in sight. He preferred to stay in his room and draw as a kid. Until he'd discovered girls. Then it was football, girls and the gym.

"So what do you want for lunch?"

"Lou's!"

"Girl after my own heart." They headed to the little shop and loaded up on yeasty bread and garlicky, sauce-laden meatball grinders. Knowing Darcy and her staff, he ordered a few extras to pass out to whoever wanted to duke it out for them. With a cooler full of sodas and ream of napkins, he let Brittany entertain him on the slow ride across town.

All the schools let out at the same time so the buses congested every main road. By the time he got to Blackstone's, his truck smelled like an Italian restaurant and his stomach was roaring.

He boxed up a half-dozen grinders and kept two out for him and his girls. They dodged customers and finally made it to the front of the store. Brit stopped so fast he almost crashed into her. The cooler top plopped to the floor. "Holy crap!"

"Cool, huh?"

"You did all this?" Her brown eyes were huge.

"Yep."

"Why doesn't our house look like this?"

Ben laughed and bumped her to get moving. "Budget."

"Yeah, this had to cost some big bucks."

"Here, let me get that for you." Jaime squatted in front of Brittany and scooped up the top to the cooler.

"Brit, this is Mrs. Suarez. Jaime, this is my niece, Brittany."

Brit maneuvered the bag until it slid down to her elbow so she could shake Jaime's hand. "Nice to meet ya."

Jaime laughed. "Nice to meet you too, *mija*. What's all this?"

"I figured you guys didn't have time to go out and get lunch so I brought a few grinders from Lou's."

Jaime tugged his collar until he bent down to where she could reach him for a smacking kiss on the cheek. "I think I love you, Gigantor."

Brit's musical laugh echoed. "Gigantor?"

"Jaime's a pip-squeak, of course I look huge to her."

Jaime took the box from him. "Your uncle is bigger than most men, *mija*."

"Not my dad. He's a little taller," her voice pitched lower, "and even wider."

"Oh yeah?"

"Hey, is Darcy around?" Ben interrupted before his chatty niece told Jaime all about John. No one would make the correlation to the guy that came into the store, but he wasn't taking any chances.

"She's covering a break."

"On the... Is she on the register?"

"Yes. You should hear her trying to bite back a growl whenever her station is on the loop."

"Loop?" Brittany asked.

One of the songs he'd programmed came on and the lights twirled around the single wall behind the register, the wreaths flashing in time to the music.

"That is so cool!"

Ben shrugged down at Jaime. "It's her favorite word."

"Well, I think it's pretty cool too. But I like Christmas."

"So which one's your girlfriend?"

Jaime bit back a laugh.

"The blonde lady over there."

"Wow, Uncle Ben, she's a hottie."

Jaime couldn't muffle her laugh this time. "Oh Ben, you're going to end up with a daughter just like her. I can see it."

"Ha ha, Jaime. That's very funny."

She took the box and cooler from him. "Thanks for thinking of us. I'll get Darcy off the registers so you can get some food into her. She hasn't stopped since she got here."

"Come on, squirt, let's go surprise her."

Darcy's back ached something fierce and if she heard *Rockin' Around the Christmas Tree* one more time there was going to be blood. She smiled at the customer in front of her. "Do you need a box for this?"

"Do you have two?"

Darcy looked at her dwindling stack but grabbed two anyway. When they were gone, they were gone. "Sure."

"Thanks." The woman gave her a weary smile. "Happy Holidays."

"Happy Holidays," Darcy parroted back. It was safer to say that then Merry Christmas. Heaven forbid they didn't celebrate the holiday.

Garlic and sauce wafted into her station. Man, if someone went to Lou's and didn't ask her if she wanted something there definitely going to be more than blood.

"Excuse me, miss?"

She would know that voice anywhere. She heard it before dreams and when she woke up. Sometimes she even heard it in her dreams. "Yes sir, one moment." She didn't turn around. Instead, she changed the register tape and refilled the bags under the counter.

He cleared his throat.

"I'll be right with you, sir." Her laughter was too close to the surface.

Ben gave her ponytail a sharp tug. "You wouldn't be ignoring a customer would you, miss?"

"Of course I wouldn't." The trill of a girl's laughter had Darcy turning around mid-tease. "Oh, you have company." She tilted her head to the side and gave Ben an I'm-going-to-strangle-you look. "You must be Brittany."

The girl was young and had tomboy stamped all over her. She was an obvious relation thanks to her brown eyes. They were all Ben's. Her sleeve was tucked into her jacket and she wore two crooked ponytails in the same shiny dark hair as her uncle's.

"So, you're my Uncle Ben's girlfriend, huh?"

Darcy's eyebrows shot up. Ben clamped his hand over Brittany's mouth and dragged her back against him. "I'm sorry, Britzilla here meant to say pleased to meet you."

Brittany tugged his hand away. "I was getting to it."

Darcy's chest ached for a reason she couldn't name. She smiled up at him. "Did you bring me something to eat, you wonderful man?"

"I am the wonderful man, and yes, there is saucy food for my saucy—er, I mean yes, for you."

Darcy laughed as Ben tried to censor his usual bawdy humor. Jaime waved from the customer service desk and Darcy logged off her register. "I could kiss you."

"I knew there was going to be kissing."

Darcy laughed and took the bag from Ben's niece. "How about I carry that for you?"

"Thanks." The little girl slid her hand into Ben's and looked up. "Can we eat now? I'm starving! And hot. It's a million degrees in here."

"I agree with both of those statements." Darcy shrugged out of her cardigan. Working near the door sometimes got cold, but as usual, the heat was way too high in the store. "Need help with your jacket?" she asked Brittany. She couldn't help but notice the empty sleeve.

Ben hadn't mentioned his niece was handicapped, but it wasn't exactly a conversation starter either.

"I got it." She pulled on a tab with an extra-fat marble on the end and shrugged out of her jacket. White straps held her arm securely across her chest.

"What happened?"

"I fell off my bike."

"Ow," Darcy said sympathetically.

"Definitely. Breaking your collarbone sucks."

Darcy frowned. The story niggled at her memory and she wasn't sure why. She swung the bag. "Well, a hoagie from Lou's should make you feel a little better."

"Anything by Lou makes everything better."

Ben smiled but the crinkles didn't fan around his eyes like they normally did. She frowned at him lightly. "Let's go to the break room and you can tell me all of your Uncle Ben's secrets."

Ben coughed and Darcy looked at him sharply. "Are you okay?"

"Fine, it's just dry in here."

She shrugged and led them both to the back. She swiped her card for the back swinging doors and punched in a code at the break room door.

"Wow, it's like a bank back here." Brittany looked around. "Is there something important back here?"

Darcy laughed. "It's just to keep curious customers out."

"I'm a customer."

Darcy clipped her badge to the girl's collar. "You're me today."

"Cool." She bustled into the break room. "Wow, you've got lockers just like I do at school!"

Ben looked down at her. "I thought we'd surprise you. I forget that she talks your ear off."

Darcy smiled. "It's okay, I like her."

"Good. It'd be really handy if my two favorite girls liked each other."

They broke out the food and Brittany told her all about Ben's more colorful clients at the tattoo parlor. Ben blushed but seemed to get into the swing of things with his niece.

She wasn't sure what was wrong with Ben, but he'd been off since that morning.

"The best was when Uncle Cesar put up this huge skull off the sign in the shop. It had red glowing eyes that he made with laser pointers. I love to give him ideas. Uncle Ben says I'm going to give him an ulcer someday."

Ben shook his head. "Not someday, squirt. Already."

She laughed as Ben stood and gathered their papers. "I need to use the men's room."

Darcy looked at Brittany. "Do you need to go?"

"I'm good."

Ben paused at the door. "I'll be right back."

"I think she'll be fine with me for a few minutes, Ben."

"Right."

Brittany turned to her. "You like my Uncle Ben, huh?"

Darcy crossed her arms over her stomach. "Yes. Is that a problem?"

"No, I think I like you. You're much nicer than any of the other girls that Uncle Ben has dated. They're usually nice to my face, but I hear them talk about me with my uncle when I'm out of the room. I mean really, don't they think I have ears?"

Darcy laughed. She knew that kids overheard things all too well. The things she'd heard through the thin walls of the small apartment when she was a kid would make a prostitute blush. "Some women don't like to share their time with kids."

"I get that. They want to do adult stuff."

And knowing Ben's particular gifts, she imagined most women did not want to deal with a child taking time away from his...talents.

"My dad thinks Uncle Ben is a bimbo magnet. But he says they're hot babes at least."

Darcy laughed. "It must be interesting to have men around all the time."

"They sometimes forget they shouldn't say stuff in front of me. Then my dad gets all red in the face and tells me to go to my room. Like it's my fault he said stuff he shouldn't."

Darcy couldn't stop smiling at the girl. Precocious didn't even cover it. "He was probably just embarrassed."

"Yeah, probably. Wanna see a picture of him?"

"Sure."

Brittany dug an iPhone out of her pocket. "I got Dad's old phone when he got a new one. It's pretty cool. Not as cool as the new phones, but better than the ones my friends have," she explained as she swiped it on.

She handled the phone better than Darcy knew how to use hers.

"Here. This was at Christmas last year." She swiped quickly. "And my birthday, and here was at Uncle Ben's opening of Luna Hart."

She went through the pictures so fast, Darcy barely got a chance to see, but she stopped and held the phone out with Ben and her father mugging for the camera with the sign behind them.

Darcy frowned. She'd never forget that face. "Brittany, what's your dad's name?"

"John. John Hartley."

FOURTEEN

BEN ENTERED THE CODE AND OPENED THE DOOR. BRITTANY WAS sitting next to Darcy and they looked good together. Cozier than he'd expected them to be after just meeting. His smile faded as he saw the cell phone in Darcy's hand. "Darcy, I can explain."

"You knew?"

"That's what I wanted to talk to you about this morning."

Brittany looked between them. "What's going on?"

"Nothing, squirt. Adult stuff."

She wrinkled her nose. "I hate when you say adult stuff."

Ben smiled tightly. "I know, but this time it really is."

"All right."

Darcy tucked a lock of Brit's messy ponytail behind her ear. "Hey, why don't we go out in the girl's department and see if we can find you a nice Christmas shirt. Does your dad take you to Mass or anything?"

Brit's eyes brightened. "Yeah, we go to Christmas Eve Mass. And I'm finally getting this stupid thing off tomorrow."

"That's great. We'll find you something pretty, how's that?"

Ben frowned. He was waiting for Darcy to rip into him, but she simply stood and ushered Brit out the door. She stopped. "We'll be talking about this when I get home."

Fuck.

He followed them out the door and grudgingly past the exit to the girl's department. It exploded with red and greens for the holidays as well as the dark colors of fall. Brit shoved her coat into his hands. "Can I get a dress, Uncle Ben?"

"Oh, Uncle Ben will be getting you whatever you like," Darcy chimed in.

Ben's jaw clicked shut. "Sure, short stuff. Get two."

Darcy folded her arms across her chest and followed Brit as she weaved in and out of the racks. The click of hangers as she searched for her size reverberated in his head.

She had four dresses, three skirts and two blouses hanging off Darcy's arm by the time Darcy convinced her to try a few on. Ben rocked back on his heels and didn't say a word. In fact, he was pretty sure Darcy was encouraging her to buy more than the two dresses.

"Do you need help in there?" Darcy called out.

"No. I'm just slow."

Darcy leaned on the door and stared daggers at him. He was a dead man. But she hadn't booted him out of the store, so there was still hope.

Please God, let there be hope.

Thirty minutes later, the girls were chattering at each other as though they'd been friends for years. And he had about one hundred dollars' worth of girl's clothing in his arms for the yes pile.

"You don't work on commission do you?"

Darcy lifted an eyebrow. "It'd be much worse if I did," she said sweetly.

He groaned but said nothing more. Twenty minutes later there was more on the pile and he was one hundred sixty-four dollars poorer. Two shopping bags weighed down each hand.

"Dad is going to flip!" Brittany slammed herself into his side. "Thank you, thank you, thank you!"

He smiled down at her. "Don't say I didn't get you anything cool for Christmas."

"I still get a Christmas present too, right?"

Ben shook his head. "Brat."

She threw him a cheeky grin full of dimples and raced ahead. "Darcy—"

"Not here, Ben. We'll talk tonight. I'm too mad right now, but we'll talk it out."

He frowned. He was waiting for the clothing rack to come for his head. He didn't get her at all. "Okay, come by after your shift."

She nodded, her arms crossed over her chest as she walked away.

The rest of the day dragged. He checked his phone every few minutes to see if there was a text from Darcy or from John. His stomach was a roiling mess by the time dinner rolled around. He'd stopped at the market for supplies.

He killed some time cutting vegetables for chicken stir-fry and popped three ibuprofen to combat the endless chatter from The Disney Channel that Brittany wouldn't turn off. Finally his phone buzzed.

DARCY

Be there in 10. Is B still there?

He tapped back the affirmative and mentioned that he made dinner. A few seconds later she typed back a simple *okay*.

He heated up his wok and set the chicken into the oil. He had no choice but to concentrate on the sizzle of the meat and the quick preparation time on the meal. "Set the table, Brit."

She ran in and shuffled out the plates and silverware he'd set out for her. "I like Darcy. You should make sure that whatever she was mad at you about earlier, you fix."

"You're way too astute, kid."

She shrugged. "I watched this show on Discovery about body language. It was pretty cool. And Darcy? She had all the signs of being really pissed at you."

"Oh yeah?"

"Yeah, the super nice words with that clipped tone? That's a good one. My teachers use that a lot."

Christ, the kid was too smart for her own good.

"And then there was the folded arms and tapping toe, and the way she wouldn't look you in the eye."

"Thanks, Brit."

"What? I'm telling you this stuff to help you. I don't want to see you sad like Daddy is all the time."

Ben pulled their meal off the burner for the sauce to thicken and hauled her in for a hug. "You're a good kid, you know that?"

"I know. Even if Daddy wants to box my ears in."

The door opened and Darcy slid in and hung up her coat. "Hey."

"Hey."

Well, at least she let herself in like she normally did. He was half expecting her to ring the damn doorbell. He went out into the living room. Her arms were across her midsection and something on the carpet was damn interesting.

Brit nudged him forward. "Uncle Ben made his awesome stir-fry."

"Oh yeah?"

Brit nodded and took Darcy's hand, dragging her into the kitchen. "Come sit down."

She passed him and he tried to grab her hand, but Darcy twisted her fingers away. He sighed and followed them into the small kitchen. He scooped their dinner out into a huge bowl and stuck two serving spoons into it, placing it in the middle of the table.

Brit made sure that they were facing each other at the table. She smiled around the vegetables and lined the snap peas around her plate like a frame. "They're my favorite, so I eat them last."

"I'm partial to the mini corn."

Brit stabbed one onto her fork and bit into it. "It's good. Uncle Ben makes the best sauce. My dad tries to make it, but he's better off with one of those meals in a bag."

Brit kept up a steady stream of chattering as Darcy picked at her food.

She answered her and ignored any conversation starters that Ben tried to initiate. The door opened again and Ben groaned as John filled the entryway.

"I thought you were going to be late."

John looked to Ben, then to Darcy, then back to Ben. Brittany cleared her plate and put it in the sink. "Thanks, Uncle Ben. I'm tired, so we're going to go home now."

John stammered out an okay and grabbed Brittany's jacket from the closet. He cleared his throat. "We have an early appointment with the doctor."

Brittany smiled and hopped in a circle to get her arm in the hole of her jacket. "I can't wait to get this stupid thing off."

Her dad smoothed a hand down her hair. "I know, kiddo. It's still going to be sore though."

"I know, but at least I can move and tie my shoes."

John leaned down and kissed her forehead. "Let's get moving. Thanks for taking care of her, Ben."

"Bye, Uncle Ben. Remember what I said."

He bent down for his hug. "I got it, squirt."

She hooked her arm around his neck. "If you break up with her I'm gonna be mad."

"You're not the only one."

"Good. Bye, Darcy! Nice meeting you. I can't wait to hang out again."

He stood to see Darcy in the doorway to the living room. "I had a great day with you too, Brittany."

Darcy came farther into the room. "John?"

John stopped at the door. His shoulders straightened before he turned around. "Yes?"

"You have a beautiful daughter. Remember that the next time you lose your temper."

John nodded and ushered Brittany out the door.

Ben turned around. "That's it?"

"What am I supposed to say, Ben? It's been weeks since he wrecked the Blackstone's tree."

"Yeah, weeks, not years. You can still press charges."

"I could. But what good would that do?"

Ben sat down on the couch. "I don't get it."

Darcy sat next to him, hugging her clasped hands between her knees. "I like your niece. And seeing what she's been able to do with that awful strap thing that holds her chest so tight, there's no way I can be mad."

There was three inches between them and he wasn't sure how to bridge the gap. "I didn't know, I swear. I wondered when you told me about it. And when Jaime gave me the details when I was doing the tree, but I didn't know for sure."

"Until?"

"Until I visited my brother a few weeks ago."

She closed her eyes. "And you didn't tell me."

"We barely had time to say hello with our schedules and I didn't want to ruin what was going on between us. I didn't even know how to bring it up. Oh hey, Darcy—remember that asshole that wrecked your store. Oh yeah. He's my big brother."

Darcy tucked her hands under her arms. "And you wanted to protect him."

"Yeah." He sighed, itching to hold on to her, even if it was just her hand. "And if he got arrested, what would happen to Brit? I mean sure, I'd take her, but she'd be so embarrassed about what he did."

Darcy leaned her shoulder into the couch and rested her head against the cushion, but still wouldn't unfold herself. She might as well have a bubble around her that screamed keep out.

He turned to her. "I know this is hard to get past, but I swear he's not normally like that. With the bills from the doctors and the extra hours to pay for them because he's so proud, he's been strung way too tight."

"And now?"

Ben shrugged. "Ever since Brit's mom left he's been angry. Having his daughter break her collarbone and there was nothing he could do for her just drove him over the edge. I wish I'd known it was that bad, I'd have kept him under wraps."

She searched his face, then laid her palm over his hand. "I'd have done the same. And if he hadn't come in and wrecked the store maybe we'd never have this."

He flipped his hand and caught hers before she could pull it back. "You're not mad?"

She shook her head. "You're probably the best man I know, Ben. I know you wouldn't do anything to hurt me on purpose. I just need some time to think about this." She slid her hand out from between his. "You lied."

His gut churned with their dinner and the acid that had been boiling up like crazy all day. "I don't want to lose you, Darcy."

"I don't want to lose you either." She stood up. "Thanks for dinner."

Ben couldn't think of anything he could do but watch her leave.

FIFTEEN

DARCY DRAGGED HERSELF INTO THE BREAK ROOM. IT WAS Christmas Eve and she'd worked fourteen-hour days for the last three days. She wasn't even sure what her name was anymore.

Two girls spoke quietly at the picnic table so she took the long table. She pressed her face into the cool metal and shut her eyes. She'd promised her mother she would sit down and talk to her that afternoon.

Her mom was feeling guilty that she and Jerry were out of town for two holidays in a row. She didn't have the heart to tell her mother that she was so tired that she was grateful.

She pulled out her phone and set it on the table, bumping up the ringer to wake her up. Just five minutes and she'd refresh a little. Her phone buzzed and trilled a moment later.

"Hey, Mom."

"Merry Christmas, baby! Did you hear Jerry too?"

She mustered up a smile, hoping it would show in her voice. "Yes, Mom, I heard him. Are you guys having fun?"

"I've never seen such blue oceans in the middle of December. It's so beautiful, Darcy."

"Make sure you take pictures."

"I think you should come with us next year."

"I think I'd get demoted if I asked for the week of Christmas off, Mom."

Her light laughter was cut with the soft caw of a bird. "Where are you guys this time?"

"Hawaii. We're on an excursion in the rainforest. It's so beautiful."

Darcy laid her cheek back on the table with the phone underneath. "I'm very jealous." She listened as her mother babbled on about how warm it was and how it rained for ten minutes at a time and then the storms disappeared. All of it sounded like heaven. And sounded like she'd never be able to see it in her lifetime.

The store was what she wanted. She'd worked hard to get to the general manager position. And if she missed cruises to tropical destinations, it was a price she was willing to pay.

Because a cruise didn't matter. Her eyes filled as she listened to her mother and stepfather banter back and forth about where they'd been and which places were more fun. She had that with Ben.

The lively chatter and the laughter.

"Mom, I met someone."

"Wait, hush, Jerry. What did you say?"

"I met someone. I'm pretty sure I'm in love with him."

"Oh honey. Really?"

"Don't sound so shocked, Mom."

"Well, I kind of am. You never let anything drag you away from that store."

She shifted until she could pillow her head in her arms. "I'm with him because of the store."

"You don't work with him do you, Darcy? Unless you're really sure you're in love and not just settling."

She huffed out a laugh. "No, Mom. It's the man that moved into my duplex actually."

"Oh." Her mother went silent a moment, then cleared her throat. "Are you talking about that man with the tattoos?"

Darcy winced. "Yes."

"Darcy, I'm so happy."

She sat up straight. "What? Really?"

"Honey, he's just what you need. I talked to him for twenty whole minutes when you got called into work and couldn't meet him with the key. Remember?"

Darcy frowned. The store was always calling her in. And once she was the store manager, she was going to find a way to make sure there were backups in place. She was not going to lose her life to the store. Not anymore.

"I love him, Mom."

"You don't know how happy that makes me, Darcy. I've been so afraid that you'd end up alone like I was for so long."

"You did the best you could, Mom."

"I know. And we'll talk more when I get home. But you make sure you don't let him go. I was lucky enough to find Jerry, but I almost screwed up and let him go."

Like mother, like daughter. "Being independent doesn't mean that we have to be alone. Remember that. Oh, and remember that they're dumb."

"Hey!"

Darcy laughed at Jerry's voice.

"I'm sorry, dear, but you can do really dumb things. So keep that in mind and forgive the little things. They don't mean much in the grand scheme."

Even lies? She was fairly sure he was going to tell her that night with Brittany, but how could she be certain? "Thanks, Mom. You guys have a really Merry Christmas with the rest of the cruise people."

"We will. I love you, honey. We'll celebrate when I get home."

"I'd like that." And for the first time, she actually liked the sound of Christmas. "I gotta go, Mom."

"Okay, I love you."

"I love you too." She turned off the ringer on her phone and stared at it for a full minute before she swiped the menu awake. She scrolled through to Ben's contact info and tapped in a message.

Her chest felt lighter. She was doing the right thing. Christmas meant possibilities and everything about Ben had been hopeful possibilities. Now to just get through the rest of the day.

CHAPTER 16

Ben stared at the text message for the fifth time.

"Uncle Ben, you can't use your phone in church."

Ben lowered his face to Brittany's and rubbed his nose with hers. "Brat."

He stuffed it back in his pocket, but he knew what it said. It wasn't like it was a difficult message to remember.

> DARCY
>
> Come find me after you're done with your family. Oh, and Ben...Merry Christmas.

He tried to pay attention to the homily at the vigil mass. Fortunately St. Mary's version of a vigil mass was ten instead of midnight. Brittany was fading against his arm, trying valiantly to keep her big dark eyes open.

By the end of the mass he was carrying her out. Neither he nor John were particularly religious, but it was a nice way to honor their mother for Christmas. Ben settled her into the backseat of John's van.

"Annual Christmas barbecue tomorrow?"

John nodded. "At least that I can help cook."

He hugged his brother. "Merry Christmas. Here's to a better year."

John returned the hug, slapping his back. "Amen to that."

Ben climbed into his truck and tapped his phone against his palm. He quickly fired back a message.

BEN

Are you still awake?

He started the engine and was halfway down the street when she replied with a simple *yes*. It was only a five-minute ride to their house but it felt interminable. He pulled up, surprised that the single tree was turned off already. Instead, five fat snowflakes hung in front of her door.

He grinned. No wires. His Darcy had put up her own Christmas decorations—solar ones. A sticky note was stuck to the back of the center star.

Come in.

He turned the knob and was surprised to see another string of lights. This time on the shelves above the small table in her entryway. They looked like mini-lanterns in brilliant greens, golds and purples. They hung from the books she had stacked on each end of the shelf.

He followed the lights on the stairs. The little battery-operated, scented lights that were so popular these days. Cinnamon and vanilla led the way up to the landing. "Darcy?"

He walked down the hallway. Another battery candle sat in front of her door. He pushed it open to see a curtain of white lights dripping from her window. He smiled. A large candleholder sat in the middle of the window with a huge red bow. This one was a real flame.

"Merry Christmas, Ben."

He turned to her voice. A small click sounded and her bed lit up. The wrought iron canopy was swagged with white panels at each corner and twinkle lights crisscrossed the top.

The woman in the center of the crimson sheets glowed from the inside out. "You bought a new bed."

"I paid handsomely for this king-sized bed. So handsomely you'll have to be my slave this summer to help me build my deck."

His smile widened. "I can do that."

She rolled onto her knees, a deep green negligee flowing around her hips, kissing the tops of her thighs. "I was thinking about what you said the other day."

He focused his attention on her face instead of his silk-over-cream present just inches away. "About what?"

"About not letting me go."

"I love you, Darcy. There's no way I'm letting you go." His boots hit the intricate scrollwork of her footboard and still she was too far away. He drew her forward, tracing his fingertips down the plunging back of her lingerie until he found petal-soft skin along the base of her spine. He trailed tiny circles in the hollow, smiling as she shivered.

Her Christmas-colored eyes misted with a light sheen of tears.

"I wanted to tell you right away." He wrapped his arms around her waist until she was flush with his chest and their foreheads touched. When a single tear trailed down her cheek, he held on tighter. "I should have told you as soon as I figured it out." He brushed his lips over the wetness, taking her salty flavor, her pain and her generosity inside. "Every day I waited felt worse than the last."

"You didn't think I'd understand?"

He smoothed a lock of burnished gold hair away from her face. "I was protecting my family, but you're my family now too. At least I want you to be."

She gripped his arms, curling her fingers into his simple white dress shirt. "I want that too. Really want that."

He caught her lips in a soft kiss, sipping from her until the salt of her tears faded and it was only them. "That day I was going to tell you. The one day we both had off. That last time with you," he gripped her sides, crushing her tighter to him, "I knew I loved you."

Desperate to taste her, to make sure she never went anywhere without him, he brought his hands up to cup her face. "When you trusted me even when I didn't deserve it, I knew I had to make things right. I don't want anything between us, Darcy. Especially lies."

She hooked her fingers around his wrists and stretched up to kiss him. "No more lies." She smiled.

"No more lies." Her hair slid around his fingers as he deepened the kiss. He knelt on the bed, stretching her out under him. With quick fingers she unbuttoned his shirt and flung his tie to the floor.

He lowered his mouth, sucking a tight little nipple through silk. "Speaking of lies."

She wrapped her leg around his hip and laughed as she arched up. "Do we have to?"

"I think someone was lying about how much she hates Christmas."

She cupped the back of his head. "I think it might have a few perks."

He laughed and drew on the other tip until matching dark spots clung to her like wet tissue paper. He blew lightly and laughed when her eyes flew open. "I think you secretly like Christmas."

She scissored strong thighs around his hips. The green silk pooled around her belly. He scored his nails over her hips, finding her bare. She nipped his lower lip and released the catch of his dress pants, scraping her teeth over his neck and pushing his pants and boxers over his ass. "I think Christmas might have a lot more possibilities with you around."

He rolled his hips into the valley of her thighs. "I told you I'd make you love Christmas."

She laughed into his kiss. "So gosh darn cocky."

"You said that word again."

She curled her arms around his neck, her laughter filling the room. "Gosh, I guess I did."

He groaned as he slid into her, the clasping perfection of her body and the love between them more than he could have ever hoped for.

If you're looking for more small town romance try our CRESCENT COVE, KENSINGTON SQUARE, or BROTHERS THREE ORCHARD series!

For character charts, reading order list across all of our series—including spoiler free versions—please visit our website at tarynquinn.com.

We appreciate our readers so much!
If you loved the book please let your friends know. If you're extra awesome, we'd love a review on your favorite book site.

Now...turn the page for a special sneak peek of FILTHY SCROOGE.

FILTHY SCROOGE

KAY

"If you don't get out on that dance floor, I'm going to kick your ass."

"I'm going, I'm going." I tugged at my short red velvet skirt. Mel had convinced me to schlep all the way to Brooklyn to go to this club, the least I could do was get my dance on. I missed it. Working seventy hour weeks had killed any extracurricular activities in my life. Starting my own company was worth it, dammit.

There'd been a time when a club had been my favorite outlet. I could lose myself in the colors, the music, the anonymity of it all. This place—Purgatory—lived up to its name in every way. It was in between in all ways that mattered. Depending on the day, the center of the huge building could be a dance club or concert venue. Outside was a sidewalk cafe with a garden straight out of England.

I could let the wilder side of me free.

I didn't have to be Kandy Kane here, with all that sugary name implied. Most of the time I loved it. Hell, I made my career around my name.

Here, I was just Kay.

I didn't have to make decisions or give orders.

I could feel a man's hands on my skin without the promise of anything more.

The lights flared, then dimmed. A wash of purple and red swirled over the crowd turning everyone the same hue—cool and hot at the same time. The lights and the dancers pulsed as the low beat of the song ebbed and flowed.

I felt an answering echo in my lower belly.

Bad sign.

"There she is."

I threw a narrow-eyed-glare at my best friend and assistant. She knew me far too well. "One dance."

Her glossy red lips lifted at one corner before she wrapped her lips around her straw. "Sure. I'll be here, drinking my courage."

"And you expect me to just go on out there?"

"Yes. Go let loose."

I flicked my heavily curled hair over my shoulder and took a deep breath. It was just like riding a bike.

I glided into the crush of people. Instinct took over as the music infused into the marrow of my bones. There was no expectation. No one knew me. So I let go. The watery undertones of the song urged my hips into soft, fluid circles. This was exactly what I needed. As usual, Mel had been right.

I found my spot in the center of the crush of people. I ignored the bump of strangers, and the dancers who thought they were far more talented than they were. I let my gaze drift to the whirling lights above me as the tension in my shoulders melted away.

My body became one with the underlying beat of the song. The heartbeat. I could find it in any piece of music. A Christmas carol, a hymn, a rap song, a country tune—it didn't matter. There was always heart to a good song.

Once I found it, everything else fell into place.

I slipped my fingers into my hair and let the dreamy music take me away. Clubs often extended the song with remixes and I chased the rhythm. My breath raced as the song built up and spun out.

Eyes were on me.

I ignored them.

Right now, I didn't want small talk, or someone grinding on my ass.

I just wanted this. The only release I could find.

The song changed to a big hit that had been reduced to a shadow of its original flavor. One that I didn't want to dance to. I raised my arms to shimmy my way through the crowd when a large hand slid along my waist. The pads of a man's fingers skimmed along the raised hem of my shirt.

Being in a club meant hands on you whether you wanted them or not. I'd broken my share of fingers when I wasn't in the mood. I lowered my hand to do just that when the guy invaded my space.

Strong thighs aligned with mine as he pushed me back toward the center of the floor.

My eyes flashed wide, met eyes the color of blue flame. An intense, unflinching stare. There was no guesswork, no teasing—just pure heat. His fingers slid around to the small of my back. His hips moved in time to my own.

He didn't hold me tight. Just enough to keep me close.

I tipped my head, curiosity riding me harder than annoyance. I shouldn't have allowed it. He was too big, too overwhelming to be the kind of man I normally danced with. I preferred fun and smiles. No harm, no foul kind of guys who didn't give me trouble when the dancing was over.

Not like this man.

His broad shoulders were encased in a fitted black shirt with another collared shirt under it in the same jet color. In fact, he was dressed in black from head to toe.

He stroked his thumb under my chin to bring my attention back up to his eyes. He didn't speak. Not that either of us could be heard over the music, but he didn't even bother with the pretense.

Just those ridiculous blue eyes burning into mine.

The song faded into one that I loved. Watery strings with a

staccato lyric to start before the drums and crashing tones filled the space. His hand grew bolder, coasted down my back to my ass, and his knee slid between my thighs.

Our gazes didn't waver.

Our bodies melted together in a sexual dance that should have been far too provocative for strangers. My heart raced and a wash of heat rushed from my thighs up to my sex. I couldn't remember the last time I'd had such a heady reaction to anyone, let alone a man who didn't know my name any more than I did his.

Did he do this often? I knew I sure as hell didn't.

I swallowed down a sudden flood of panic. I glanced around us. No one was paying attention to us.

His thumb was at my chin again, dragging my gaze back to his.

"Right here," he mouthed.

I swallowed and tried to step back. He brought his hand to my hip and caught my hand with his other, lacing our fingers. His skin was smooth with a ridge of calluses along his palm. The beat of the song was harder, darker than the previous ones played.

I moved into him this time.

Maybe I didn't want the link broken. Just for a few more moments.

The tingle along my thighs grew with each brush of his. The roll of his hips in time to the song changed the simple buzz to a surge. My nipples throbbed and my thighs were soaked under my skirt. Arousal slammed into me. Panic licked along my lower spine and activated my flight response.

Dancing was one thing. More?

No, that wasn't me.

I twisted away and pushed my way through the dancers. The murmur of pissed off people doubled. The next song was a Britany remix that had the room pulsing again.

My heart crashed in my ears as I finally broke free from the dance floor.

Don't do it. Don't turn around.

But I couldn't help myself. I glanced back to see if my mystery man was following, but he was not.

He'd probably moved on to the next girl.

So stupid. He'd probably lost interest the moment I'd pulled back like a frightened virgin.

Worldly. Yeah, that was me.

I might know how to find my inner dancing queen, but the vixen half of me had yet to figure out how to play.

I placed my hand over my midriff. Everything was still buzzing and fluttering madly. I tugged my shirt down, then smoothed my skirt. Disappointment crashed into self-preservation.

Besides, there was no way I could test the waters with someone like that. I was better off with Jason. He was one of my temps at work. He'd been asking me out for the last three weeks. He was sweet and would undoubtedly take his time—and surely let me take mine.

I'd been putting him off because he was my employee, but the season was officially over tomorrow. At least the Christmas season, which pretty much floated most of my business for the year. Maybe if he asked me again, I'd have to just say yes for once.

Eyes the color of blue flame flashed into my head. Intense eyes. Hooded eyes with slashing cheekbones, giving his face arresting angles.

A man like that didn't seem nice. He'd take and demand.

Damn if that didn't give me a serious pause.

No. I shook my head firmly—not for me. The Jasons of the world were more my speed. My fingernails dug into my palms. I couldn't even pull Jason's face up at the moment. Kind brown eyes...maybe? Or were they hazel?

I straightened my shoulders and headed for the bar.

Those damn blue eyes were sticking. I had little doubt they'd follow me into my dreams tonight. Time to find Mel and get the hell out of here. I had a huge day ahead of me tomorrow anyway.

I could trust work.

I understood work.

Just one more day to get through.

NOW AVAILABLE!

Check out our website at taryquinn.com.

CHECK OUT OUR OTHER HOLIDAY TITLES

Desperately Seeking Kitty

Fiancée By Christmas

CEO Daddy

Mistletoe Baby

Filthy Scrooge

Saving Kylie

Unwrapped

Find out more details on our website

tarynquinn.com.

QUINN AND ELLIOTT

Rockers Reading Order

Lost in Oblivion

Winchester Falls

Found in Oblivion

Hammered

Rock Revenge

Brooklyn Dawn

Other Series

Tapped Out

Love Required

Boys of Fall

ABOUT TARYN QUINN

USA Today bestselling author, ***TARYN QUINN,*** is the sexy and funny alter ego of bestselling authors Taryn Elliott & Cari Quinn. We've been writing together for years, but we have decided to pull the trigger on a combo name just for fun.

And so...Taryn Quinn was born!

Do you like ultra sexy small town romance full of shenanigans? Quirky office romances full of steam? Okay, look...we pretty much just love writing steamy stories. If you're all about that, we're your girls!

For more information about us...
tarynquinn.com
tq@tarynquinn.com

facebook.com/TarynQuinn

x.com/TQauthor

instagram.com/tarynquinnauthor

tiktok.com/@tarynquinnromance

www.ingramcontent.com/pod-product-compliance
Lightning Source LLC
Chambersburg PA
CBHW060440180626
46817CB00007B/2907